CW00402773

FREEDOM PLEDGE

Adventures of a Victorian Soldier - Prequel

M. J. TWOMEY

M.J.Twomey

Copyright © 2020 by M. J. TWOMEY

All rights reserved.

No part of this book may be reproduced in any form or by any electronic or
mechanical means, including information storage and retrieval systems, without
written permission from the author, except for the use of brief quotations in a
book review. Unauthorized distribution or use of this text may be a direct
violation of the author's rights and those responsible may be liable in law
accordingly.

eBook ISBN: 978-1-954224-06-3

FIRST EDITION

M.J.Twomey

Visit my website to join the mailing list for information on new releases and updates.

www.mjtwomey.com

WARNING

This book is a work of fiction. Any scenes with actual people from these historic times are fiction. The place names used reflect names from the nineteenth century.

MAP OF CRIMEA, 1854

CHAPTER ONE

September 14, 1854, Calamita Bay, Crimea

Sleek frigates, three-decked warships, and lumbering transports crowded into Calamita Bay to land their cargoes of men, horses, and equipment for the allied attack on the Russian naval base at Sevastopol, some twenty-five miles to the south, and the Russians failed to oppose them. Black-hulled steamers towing fat merchantmen to their anchorages vomited greasy smoke into the blue autumn sky, and Royal Navy frigates churned the Black Sea to a creamy froth as they circled the fleet like guard dogs and worried the stragglers into line.

On the deck of *Himalaya*, a three-masted steamship, Samuel gagged at the reek from the cholera corpses floating in the bay. "Poor buggers. May God have mercy on their souls," he murmured, casting his gaze to the heavens. "And damn the inept aristocrats who stranded the army for so long in disease-plagued Bulgaria." He raised his voice so William could hear him. "I can't believe it. There must be three or four hundred ships here."

William nodded. "Odd, yes, with former enemies united against Russia. Who'd have thought we'd be fighting alongside the frogs when Waterloo wasn't that long ago. And those Ottomans? I'm sure there's more to this alliance than what they tell us. I don't even know why we're fighting. All I know is that the press and every man on the street back home started howling for Russian blood, and next thing we poor sods are out here suffering disease and bad food because corrupt quartermasters stole the best of it back in England."

Padraig had read old newspapers that the officers had left around the boat and regurgitated the news to Samuel, insisting they shouldn't fight without understanding the reason, so Samuel took the opportunity to impress his captain.

"The tsars have been expanding Russia at the expense of Turkey's waning empire for decades, and Tsar Nicholas is using the excuse of protecting religious freedom and his Balkan subjects to lunge for control of the Bosphorus and Dardanelles Straits. His real reason is to give his warships in Sevastopol access to the Mediterranean. Of course, the resulting threat to British commerce with India and other nations terrifies their high-and-mighty lordships back in London." Samuel imitated Lord Lucan's accent to add, "Such is intolerable when Britain rules the waves. British affluence, power, and prestige depend on preserving our overseas trade. The Mediterranean Sea lanes will remain free from Russian domination."

William pushed a lock of hair off his face. "What has trade to do with religion?"

"Nicholas invaded Moldavia and Wallachia, claiming to protect Orthodox Christians from persecution. When he ignored all ultimatums to withdraw, Britain, France, and Turkey allied against Russia. Since we made a hash of punishing Russia for crossing the Danube and idled for months in Bulgaria, when some idiot called for attacking Sevastopol, every preacher with a soapbox on a London street corner took up the cry. So here we are, embarked on another useless exercise."

William frowned and glanced around. "You really shouldn't speak like that, cousin. Your Anglo-Irish countrymen already scorn your family for such radical thinking, and they come from the same background. Your father's estate in Cork won't save you if a vengeful Crown comes after you."

"Radical? The indifference of the Anglo-Irish ruling class to the starvation, sickness, and suffering of their Catholic tenants disgusted my family. It should disgust you too. Their greed—exporting all the produce harvested in Ireland, leaving nothing for their tenants to eat, driving people from their homes, and tearing the roofs from over their heads during the famine—killed thousands." Samuel offered his snuffbox to William. "Fine stuff. I got it in London." He took a pinch after William had helped himself and savored the kick. "Someone must speak out against it. You live in England, so you've no idea what it was like, but you must accept all men are equal in the eyes of the Lord. The Irish should follow the Americans and break away from the empire."

"*Lieutenant*." William tugged Samuel farther from the nearest officers and peered around again. "That's close to treason."

Samuel scrubbed a hand across his face. "Sorry. The bigotry of the aristocrats riles me. I'll say no more." He *was* sorry. He hadn't intended to drag William into a discussion of Irish independence. At least not on the deck of a converted steamer ferrying hundreds of Her Majesty's troops.

William placated himself with a pinch from his own silver snuffbox, extended the box to Samuel like a peace offering, and changed the subject. "Did you see how the French handle their boats; we were lucky more didn't collide. And Lord Raglan rewards them by letting the buggers land first. At this rate we won't get ashore for days. How will the horses bear it? The poor beasts have languished head-to-head in their stalls with no space to lie down for five days now. We already lost twenty-six on the voyage from Queenstown to Constantinople. I shudder to think how many died on this leg."

William plucked at his neat black beard, a habit he fell into when his thoughts scattered. He was quite a few years older than

Samuel—thirty-five, if Samuel remembered correctly—but fit for his age. And he stood tall even when no one was watching. Height ran in their family, and William used his height to press his authority as commander of C Company. Samuel was three inches taller, and he'd learned from William. As a growing boy who never stopped growing, he'd tried to hide his height. Now, as William's senior lieutenant, he stood tall, taking advantage of every inch.

"I can't speak to how fit the horses will be, but we've lost none so far." Samuel rolled his shoulders. And he intended that they wouldn't lose any before the battles began. "The troopers bathed the animals' noses with vinegar and water, and that got them to eat. I'm going to check on Goldie in a moment."

Samuel raised his brass spyglass and glassed the narrow, four-mile stretch of beach and the salt lakes behind it that divided the beach from the crescent of turfy downs ending in reddish sandstone cliffs to the south. The French were scrambling ashore from rafts, the blue uniforms of the infantry demure beside the scarlet pantaloons, the blue tunics, and the red burnooses of France's chasseurs, the Zouaves, and the Spahis from North Africa. They were already erecting colored tents at measured distances along the beach to designate the separate landing points for the infantry divisions of Canrobert, General Pierre Bosquet, and Prince Napoleon.

"The frogs seem handy enough now that their anchors are down," Samuel said. "They've disembarked their three divisions already and are landing their big guns from those artillery rafts." He cursed under his breath when he discovered he was sucking on his cheek—William wasn't the only one with a nervous habit —and checked the sky. The weather had been good, but the clouds stacking on the horizon would make for a lumpy sea. "I don't think we're going to have it so easy."

William rubbed his hands down his navy-blue trousers. "Don't I know . . . Winching the horses into the barges and swimming them ashore will be downright dangerous when the winds shift."

Samuel realized he was tapping his foot and stopped. "I'll risk the sea, anything to get off this boat, and I'm sure the horses feel the same way."

Foraging French soldiers were returning to the beach with firewood and food, and Samuel's mouth watered at the sight. "Mmm . . . What I wouldn't give for a roasted chicken or duck."

". . . horses in the surf. Are you listening?"

"I beg your pardon, dear William. I was just thinking about roasted fowl. I'm sick of salted beef and wine that's turned to vinegar."

"No chance of that; the frogs will have stripped the land bare by the time we land." William held out his hand. "Lend me your spyglass."

Samuel wiped his sweat off the spyglass and passed it over. "You were saying we need to land before the weather turns. I agree. It'll be brutal on the horses if that surf picks up."

"It beats me why the Russians failed to defend the beach; artillery could have swept the French from the bay before they reached shore." William scanned the beach with the spyglass.

"First we anchored at of Eupatoria, then we sailed east down here," Samuel said. "And if Raglan himself couldn't decide where he was landing, what hope had the Russians of guessing where our fleet was headed?" A pink reflection glittered on the low hills. A dozen dark and bearded men with shaggy hats sat on rangy horses with the setting sun twinkling on their lances. "Russkies, by golly. Do you think they're Cossacks?"

"Where? Let me see." William swiveled the glass. "I daresay they are. Ragged-looking beggars, eh? Nothing but ill-bred peasants. Take a look."

Accepting the spyglass, Samuel bit his tongue and fixed the lens to the Cossacks in their brown greatcoats. William was a fine fellow, but he could be as arrogant as an aristocrat. Samuel had once yearned for a title; what Anglo-Irish man didn't? But the cruelty and greed of aristocrats during the famine in Ireland had turned him against them.

So these were the ferocious irregulars of lore, the Cossacks . . . They looked nothing special to him. "Raglan should have landed the cavalry first. The Seventeenth would have chased those buggers away in a jiffy."

William pushed off the guardrail. "Well, *I'm* going ashore to secure the regiment a decent patch before the frogs hog all the suitable spots. Look after the lads while I'm gone."

"See if you can find us a fowl or two. I'm off to check on Goldie." Samuel pocketed his spyglass and headed for the companionway.

Gulls wheeled and shrieked above, diving for scraps thrown overboard by the cook's helpers. The birds reminded Samuel of the seagulls soaring in from the bay across Springbough Manor— and he sighed. He missed Father and Jason and Emily.

He tried to imagine Jason next to him on the rolling water, smiling at the image. Jason was no fighting man. But he didn't have to be. He'd inherit the family estate and continue Father's successful management. Samuel's smile grew when next he pictured Emily striding aboard a ship. She was only three years older than Samuel, but she'd try to mother him, even among the troops.

He shook his head even as he walked the crowded deck. No, he couldn't think such things about her. She'd always dusted him off when life tripped him up; she was generous and tempered her corrections with kindness. They were a close-knit family, never happy unless they were meeting one another. He missed them dearly and knew that they thought of him and prayed for him daily. But they weren't with him now, and he had better concentrate on what was happening on the ship.

The officers had the best vantage points on the bow and the stern, while the troopers were crammed in the ship's waist between the two idle masts. The men were fidgeting and grumbling down there, eager to get ashore, and the noncommissioned officers were pushing them about and shouting for order.

The clatter of horses fighting and kicking in cramped stalls drew him back from his reverie, the cacophony ringing up from below deck accompanied by the funk of grease and horse dung, and he ground his teeth. Bloody commanders should have allowed the horses off first. Poor Goldie.

Padraig, his childhood friend, stood with Trooper Price by the companionway, watching the rafts and tenders shuttling between the boats and the beach. They were likely judging the men's efficiency and skill, finding both to be lacking.

Price spat over the gunwale. "Look at that lickspittle Lawrence sucking up to old Bloodyback and Lucan. What a circus."

Samuel pretended not to hear Price. The pugnacious Liverpudlian was a good lancer and didn't deserve a flogging for saying what Samuel also thought.

In one cutter, wearing full dress uniform—sabers and all—stood Colonel Lawrence, commander of Samuel's Seventeenth Lancers; Lieutenant-General James Brudenell, seventh Earl of Cardigan and commander of the Light Brigade; and General Bingham, third Earl of Lucan and overall commander of the British cavalry, with Lawrence bobbing his head like a bird, almost bowing to the generals.

Price blushed and saluted clumsily. "Sir." Samuel held back his smile when he saw Price's discomfort. Perhaps the tough soldier would learn to watch his mouth.

"Good afternoon, sir." Padraig snapped off a smart salute.

"Idling? Shall I ask the sergeant major to find you something to do?"

"No, sir. I've me jobs, I have," Price said gruffly, his accent stronger than usual. "I'm just on me way. Excuse me, please, sir." Price saluted again and scampered to the companionway.

"And you, Corporal," Samuel snapped in his parade ground voice. "Have you no work to do?"

Padraig glanced around before answering him in Spanish. "Ah, don't be a fucker. Do you blame Pricey? I've never seen such a muster of peacocks."

María Kerr, Padraig's Spanish mother, was married to Jerry, manager of the Kingston's estate, and had wet-nursed the boys together when Samuel's mother had died in childbirth. They were brothers in all the ways that counted but miles apart in a British army where commoners—especially Catholics—seldom held a commission and in a society where Anglo-Irish Protestants considered Irish Catholics to be superstitious, intemperate, and indolent. The army forbade officers from fraternizing with enlisted men; therefore Samuel had appointed Padraig his orderly so they could look after each other, at the same time providing Padraig useful perquisites. So far each had kept the other alive and relatively injury-free through campaigns in India and Burma.

"Let's have a look at them, then." Samuel took out his spyglass and glassed the senior officers in the cutter.

Ruddy-faced Lawrence, second Earl of Sligo, looked more like a well-fed farmer than a cavalryman, and his feeble whiskers looked like an untidy butcher had plucked them. Samuel pinched his lips when he moved on to Lucan. For some reason unknown to Samuel, General Bingham held a grudge against him and had blocked his promotion twice. Bastard.

Samuel huffed and kept his lens centered on Lucan, who was looking down his long nose at Lawrence. Lucan was fit for a man in his midfifties, but everything about him hinted at conceit: his rigid posture, the immaculate gray beard, and the gold ropes looped across his breast and covering the cuffs of his cobalt frock coat. Lucan was an Anglo-Irishman like Samuel, but Samuel despised him for ordering mass evictions in the west of Ireland during the Great Famine. Irish Catholic peasants reviled him and called him the Exterminator, but the Anglo-Irish, those who'd welcomed the famine that cleared the land of countless Irish peasants, admired him.

Samuel turned his attention to the other general. No doubt Lieutenant-General Brudenell had quaffed champagne and slept in a feather bed on his luxury yacht all the way across the Black Sea, with nary a thought for his suffering cavalrymen. Cardigan was lean, with a long face and pork chop sideburns billowing like sails in the ocean breeze. He was typical of the incompetent aristocrats filling the army's top ranks. Lucan and Cardigan were stiff-lipped and tense, looking anywhere but at each other.

"Would you look at those idiots?" Samuel chuckled and handed the spyglass to Padraig. "Lucan's married to Cardigan's sister, and Cardigan believes he cheats on her. Cardigan's no one to talk. The randy old goat has dropped his trousers for every loose woman in London. William heard that countless times at the Army and Navy Club in London."

"I didn't figure Captain Morris for a gossip. I thought your cousin was a saint." Padraig focused the spyglass. "The boatload of them are as useful as a chocolate teapot; may the Blessed Virgin save us from the lot of them."

"How's Goldie?"

"I just looked in on her. She's fine, considering. She's lost weight and looks down, but she'll perk up as soon as she gets ashore." Padraig handed back the spyglass.

"Good. I'll visit her, anyway. I miss the old girl."

Padraig opened his mouth, paused, and then glanced furtively around. "You need to hear this." He spoke quietly and in Spanish. "That prick, Maxwell, is acting strangely. He was flashing the shore with a signal mirror this morning and gave me a dirty look when he noticed I saw him. I don't know . . . Something's off about him."

Samuel's head pulsed as memories from the days of his bleak life in boarding school stabbed at him. The classroom—where the sons of the privileged sat on hard wooden desks arrayed in straight rows before a pontificating teacher, learning by rote, reciting words from the Classics, and speaking ill of Irish Catholics—had been bad. And he'd loathed the fagging system so highly prized by Victorian society to teach boys something of service. Fagging created a progressive social structure in the school that virtually gave senior boys total power over younger boys, and bullies frequently abused that power.

And one of those bullies had crossed halfway around the world with Samuel.

When Samuel shivered, he turned the movement into a shrug, not willing for Padraig to see his instinctive reaction.

Five years older than Samuel, who'd just turned twenty-one, Viscount Ian Maxwell had made his life miserable because he and many other students considered the Kingstons traitors to their privileged class when Samuel's father publicly condemned the Anglo-Irish landowners for their cruel treatment of their Catholic tenants during the famine.

He hadn't stopped making Samuel's life miserable.

Getting ashore would already be difficult enough; he refused to clash with the well-connected captain. "I'm sure it's nothing; perhaps he was gaffing about."

"That lout? Ha." Padraig pounded on the gunwale. "And it's not the first time he's done it. I saw him using the mirror back in Varna too."

Samuel ran a hand through his hair, taking the time to unsnarl a few wind-tied knots to give himself a chance to think. That was indeed strange, but Maxwell was a captain and an aristocrat; Samuel couldn't challenge him. "Ah, I . . . I'll mention it to William and see what he thinks. He's gone ashore; I'll tell him when he returns. Do you want to come see Goldie with me?"

"It's foul down there, but why not?"

Padraig wasn't exaggerating about the stench; it was appalling. Poor Goldie. Samuel pinched the skin at his throat as he ducked through the low doorway into the gloom. But worse were the dangers that awaited them ashore. Thousands of entrenched Russians and cannons crouched like predators behind the stone walls of Sevastopol, ready to rain death upon the allied army.

———

Himalaya had lain at anchor for four days, and finally the regiment was disembarking. Thirty lancers from C Company struggled to calm their horses on the rolling deck, their pale faces burning in the autumn sun. Even the freshening wind failed to shift the rancid stench of damp serge, sweat, and dung. The forlorn whinnies and the ring of steel horseshoes were out of place on the stirring sea.

Would the officers ever get a move on and order them ashore? Samuel tilted his head back and studied the brassy sky. Three days of rising to the expectation of getting off that stifling tub followed by three days of standing around all day going nowhere had drained him. And he at least had the small comforts of an officer—more space and better food. It must have been hell for the troopers crammed amidships and worse yet for the horses penned down below. If he didn't get off today, he'd go crazy.

The chink of Goldie's bit drew Samuel's attention back to the palomino standing with Padraig, and he winced at her dull gold coat and splayed legs. "*Pobrecita*. I should have left her back in Clonakilty; this campaign's been hell on the horses."

"Are you mad?" Padraig stroked Goldie, instantly earning him a soft whinny. "She's the finest charger in the Light Brigade. If you'd left her at home, you'd be as bad as me—stuck with a Syrian mule. I don't know why that braggart Nolan bought those beasts for the troopers. Cheap, I'd wager. It wasn't worth the navy's time ferrying horses from Britain down to Bulgaria." He continued to run one hand over Goldie, soothing her. "I sure wish I had Rogue here. Silly regulation that only officers can ship their own nags. Save them a bit of coin if they didn't have to buy animals everywhere we go."

Samuel pictured the ridiculous image of a lancer charging into battle on a mule and hid his smile at Padraig's irreverent croaking, complaints that would have landed Padraig at the knotted end of the lash years ago if his superiors understood what he was saying. Samuel shifted Padraig aside and patted Goldie. "If anything happens to her, I'll be devastated." Her soft, spikey hair tickled the pad of his palm, and her silky nostrils flared, puffing warm breath over him.

"Of course you would be." Padraig shifted and looked toward land. "That wretch, Maxwell, is holding us back out of malice. I told you he was angry that I saw him with a signal mirror. What did Captain Morris say about him?"

"Damnation, I forgot. William stayed ashore that night, and it slipped my mind. I'll tell him as soon as I see him."

"See that you do. I don't trust that bastard. He wasn't signaling for the good of his health. Not unless he was lining up a whore to tup when we get ashore."

Padraig could be dramatic, especially when his dislike of aristocrats colored his suspicions. But dislike was hardly a reason to stir up problems with a man like Maxwell. "I will. Now stop rhyming." Damnation, it was time to get off the boat, but the rafts were taking forever. Samuel glassed the beach.

Two rafts were bobbing on the swelling combers with four flagging sailors paddling hard for *Himalaya,* and beyond them horses reared and bucked in the surf as dragoons tried to coax them onto the beach. The army hadn't shipped carts to transport supplies or even the sick and wounded, and the cavalry's first mission would be to steal transport from the surrounding countryside. Thousands of blue-jacketed Frenchmen loitered on the beach, too many of them staggering or lying listlessly, crippled from cholera. The British were still landing on the north side, where redcoats and the riflemen in bottle-green jackets had formed a defensive line to keep the lurking Cossacks at bay.

Samuel and Padraig watched all afternoon, increasingly impatient as sailors winched horses over the side of the ship and lowered them thrashing and squealing onto the rafts. What began as heavy rain soon deteriorated into a storm that swept over the armies on the beach and battered the ships in the bay.

Padraig's shoulders slumped, and he pulled at the collar of his sodden tunic. "Well, that's it. Nobody in their right mind would try to unload a horse now."

"C Company next, Lieutenant Kingston." Captain Maxwell sneered as he beckoned Samuel forward. "You men, step aside and let them through while I check the raft." His peaked brows and narrow gray eyes gave him a hawkish appearance, and his body was sluggish as he moved to the steamer's open entry port, where the sea churned nastily not far below.

Samuel pressed his lips together. The lout was still a bully, and Samuel still didn't want to tangle with him, yet the sea was getting dangerous, and he should ask Maxwell to wait until morning. He thumbed his ear, quickly running through likely repercussions of the simple request. Maxwell would make his life hell if he delayed the landing. His stomach knotted.

He had to get over his fear of men like Maxwell, and he had to report Maxwell's suspicious behavior to William the next time he saw him. It was unfair that such men rose in the ranks purely by virtue of their pedigree. He stroked Goldie's shivering neck while Padraig fitted the sling around her belly, and she nuzzled him for an apple. But she was out of luck. Even the officers had no fruit, though they still had fresh bread and meat every day, faring better than the men who choked on rotting salt meat, gin, and barrels of peas dated as far back as 1828.

"There you are, old girl, sound as a pound." Padraig *tsked* and frowned at the towering white caps breaking over the gray sea. "I don't like this at—"

"Stop griping, Kerr, and get that beast in the air." Maxwell climbed back through the entry port. "You may be a corporal, but you can still get the lash." He raked Samuel with his gaze, daring him to intervene.

What a churl. But now wasn't the time to challenge him. Samuel would go through the chain of command. "I'll go down to meet her at the raft, Corporal."

They called it a raft, but thank God the craft was more solid than a typical raft with a flat bottom and high gunwales to keep out the waves. They'd lower the forward ramp when they reached the beach. Visibility was only five feet in the dying light by the time Goldie and five more mounts stood quivering in the raft where Padraig and a handful of Samuel's troopers clung to their bridles.

Sergeant Major Wagner spat a wad of tobacco over the side and scowled. "This is madness, sir. Is Captain Maxwell trying to kill us? This raft is— Here comes another horse, goddamn it."

Another horse's hooves dropped through the driving rain, and Samuel shouted up through his bullhorn as the raft rose four feet and crashed against *Himalaya's* towering hull. "Easy, easy. Another three feet."

No, Wagner was right—this was madness. "Belay that. Winch this horse back on board. Take them all back. It's insanity to t—"

Snap!

The rope suspending the black mare parted, and she fell with a pitiful scream. She thumped the gunwale, the raft tilted precariously, and the mare splashed into the boiling sea. The other horses threw up their heads and scrambled to keep their feet, hooves hammering the deck.

"Blessed Virgin," Padraig roared as he hauled on the reins of the chestnut mare sidestepping beside him. "What the devil's going on?"

"That's my horse." Price threw himself to the gunwale and peered over the side. "Poor thing. I'll kill them for this."

The bow line sprang free, and the raft whipped away from *Himalaya's* plunging hull. A second later the last rope holding the raft to the ship parted with a *twang*, just missing Sergeant Major Wagner. A nine-foot wave lifted the raft and hurled it into the gathering gloom.

Samuel's stomach clenched, and he hugged Goldie's wet head. "We're adrift. My God, we're adrift. Paddles, quick. Find paddles. Padraig, you're the sailor. Rig a sail on this thing, goddamn it."

"Jamie, hold my horse." Padraig passed his reins to Jamie Begley and balanced on the rolling deck as he hurried to the mast. A moment later he called out, "Someone cut the halyards, Lieutenant. Bloody idiot."

Sabotage? But that was impossible; surely there was another explanation.

"No paddles either, sir." Sergeant Major Wagner's round face was ashen. Samuel had never seen the Prussian pale, not even when facing a horde of Burmese irregulars, but there on the savage sea, he was lost.

"Maxwell. It was Maxwell. The rat threw out the paddles and sabotaged the rigging." Padraig spoke rapid Spanish, hiding his suspicions from the others.

Samuel didn't have time to dwell on Maxwell. Besides, Padraig was wrong about him. *The man was a viscount.*

He ducked as a wave crashed over the gunwale, and the icy cold water instantly had him shivering. The horses were kicking and throwing their heads up in the makeshift stalls, their eyes rolling white as the raft careened through the sheeting rain. "Calm the horses and break off the seats; we'll use them as paddles." He kicked at the plank that served as a seat beside him.

"Right, sir, I've a paddle now." Adam Price waved a broken seat in the air like a prize. He was a rough type from Liverpool, with lumps on his prominent forehead and a misshapen nose that had been broken too many times. "But which way do I paddle?"

Before Samuel could answer, another wave slammed over the raft, spinning it like a cork in a drain and blinding the men. Samuel sagged onto the seat he'd failed to kick free as the twinkling lanterns of the fleet disappeared in the curtain of rain. It was hopeless. They could no more steer the raft than they could swim for shore. "Leave it, Price. Just hang on tight and keep the horses calm."

Padraig had his knife out and was cutting up a sail.

"What are you doing, Padraig? We'll need that when the storm dies down."

"We won't survive the storm unless we steady the boat." Padraig's voice was barely audible above the screams of the horses and the creak of the timbers as waves pounded the raft. "I'm making a drogue to steady the raft."

Samuel hadn't a clue what a drogue was, but Padraig had helped on the fishing boats back in West Cork before taking the Queen's shilling. He'd also read every book in Springbough Manor's library. If the corporal had a plan, it was probably a good one.

Pitching and plunging, the raft spun through rain and darkness with the horses screaming and the men praying or cursing. A towering structure loomed out of nowhere, and the raft bounced off the ship. Samuel held his breath as the raft scraped along the hull with a harrowing screech. Kiely, a young trooper from Kerry, tried to fend off the hull, and razor-sharp barnacles slashed his hand. Faint shouts sounded from the deck of the towering ship, and a row of indistinct, peering faces far above flashed briefly before disappearing into the dusk.

Two waves slammed together beneath the raft, and her flat bottom creaked as she rose high on the swell and shot clear of the ship.

Samuel braced, holding tight as the raft yawed and sawed into the spray-lashed darkness.

"There you go, my beauty." Padraig heaved a bundle of sail and rope over the stern. Seconds later the rope twanged taut, and the raft shuddered, throwing Samuel off balance. The raft steadied, still tossing, but no longer spinning and yawing.

"'Tis my drogue," Padraig shouted. "My sea anchor. It's holding us steady. Now all we do is ride out the storm."

"Ride it out, he says," Price grumbled. "All the way across the

Black Sea, or worse, we'll end up back in fucking Varna, a hole that stinks worse than an Irish village."

"Well, it never stank as bad as the tarts you galloped back in Liverpool," Padraig said with a grin.

After buttoning down the lapels of his field service jacket against the cold, Samuel drew his cloak tight, all the while pretending not to hear the bickering. Soldiers griped and joked to keep their spirits up, and in that desperate plight, they needed all the lift they could get. "Do what you can to keep your powder dry lads and try to get some rest." He sagged against Goldie, and his hands fell at his sides. Get some rest? He was fooling nobody. They'd drown at sea or drift into the arms of the Russians.

It didn't help when the rain stopped late that night, because the raft bucked and heaved without pause, soaked by an ocean of green that chilled Samuel to the bone and hammered the lancers into shivering silence.

They'd need the luck of the angels to survive the night. Samuel looked at his haversack on the deck. His mother's old Bible was in there, but it was too wet and dark to take it out to read. He pulled out his compass and squinted, but he couldn't see the needle. He'd no idea where they were headed. His lips moved unbidden. "God the Father in heaven, have mercy on us. God the S . . ."

CHAPTER TWO

September 18, dawn

By dawn the storm had blown out, leaving a white-capped sea that rolled and pitched the raft without regard. The coastline gradually materialized from the morning haze, a low profile climbing into a great bluff rising hundreds of feet above the sea.

Samuel stirred his soaked body, rummaged in his haversack for his spyglass, and glassed the coast. It seemed the wind was blowing them south. He'd faced trials in Burma, that was for sure, but nothing like this—drifting behind enemy lines with the rigging sabotaged. His shoulders dropped. If only Jerry Kerr were there; the veteran sergeant major would have known what to do. But Jerry would have said *Step up, Samuel, lad, you're in command now, and these boy, and my Padraig all depend on you.*

On board *Himalaya*, he'd studied maps for hours, and he now concluded he was staring at the cliffs beside the Alma River.

"Dozed off, did you?" Padraig looked up from reeving a rope through a block. "I reckon the storm blew us south of the fleet."

The man had the unerring instincts of a born sailor. Samuel never doubted him.

"Yes. I believe those are the cliffs beside the Alma River. And if that's the case, the storm blew us some twenty miles south." He waited for Padraig to meet his eyes. "Behind enemy lines."

"Well then, we'll be the first into Sevastopol." Padraig winked, switched to Spanish, and added, "Long before Lord Raglan and his bumbling generals." Padraig patted the sail beside him. "A pity I cut a swath of the sail for my sea anchor, but desperate times need desperate measures and all that, eh? Anyway, I jury-rigged the rest of the sail. She won't sail close to the wind, but we can take on this northerly breeze and probably land just south of that headland." He pointed.

"We can't sail back to the fleet?"

"Not with this wind."

Samuel scratched the stubble on his chin as he looked north to where the distant haze hid the fleet. If memory served, there was a road down the coast to Sevastopol that crossed four rivers: the Bulganak, the Alma, and . . . he couldn't remember the names of the other two. But if he guessed right, the raft lay offshore close to where the Alma flowed east to west into the Black Sea. The land north of the Alma was flat, mainly corn-fields and orchards, and even if the Russians guarded the road, perhaps they could sneak past in the fields. "Then we must slip through the enemy lines." He scanned the haversacks piled along the gunwales. Thank goodness they'd loaded them first. Each haversack contained a trooper's cartridge box with powder, lead balls, and percussion caps for the Colts—the Russians were in for a surprise when they faced the revolu-tionary new six-shooters. Their lances were stacked along the gunwales too. At least they were well armed. He nudged the nearest man with his boot. "Hoffman, help Corporal Kerr with that sail."

Ebenezer Hoffman's long worn face made the gaunt man look older than his twenty-five years. Rumor had it that bailiffs caught him poaching and the magistrate made him choose between prison and the army. A persistent complainer, he muttered under his breath as he brushed back the stringy hair plastered across his eyes and stirred himself slowly.

"Best not backtalk the lieutenant, you bastard," Sergeant Major Wagner growled at Hoffman from the stern, "or I'll whip you and toss your scarred arse overboard."

"Hold on, mate." Padraig pointed to the taut line that disappeared into the sea. "Let's have that drogue in first, if you would, Sergeant Major, and someone take the tiller until I haul the sail."

Having set the sail and got the raft underway, Padraig took the tiller. "The raft is drifting sideways almost as much as she's going forward, but sure it's the best I can do. Would you join me back here, Lieutenant, please?"

The horses were quiet, shivering upright in their crude stalls as Samuel made his way aft. His wet clothes were stiff and salty, and his legs ached from sitting on a hard seat all night. He only knew Goldie. Captain Louis Nolan's men had delivered the other horses from Syria, and the men had had little time to ride them. Only God knew how they'd hold up, but they looked shook after their voyage across the Black Sea. Their rough night in the raft wouldn't have helped either. Worse, Price would have to ride doubled up behind one of the others.

He nodded at Jamie Begley, who held a canvas pail to the muzzle of a dazed bay mare. "Well done, Begley. You'd the sense to trap rainwater in the buckets last night." Nobody knew more about horses than that man. A slight fellow, so maybe he didn't intimidate the horses. Samuel could never guess his age—older than Jason, who was twenty-eight, and younger than Father, who was in his midforties. Kiely, the youngest trooper in C Company, was leaning against the rail that penned the horse allocated to him back in Varna, his bloodshot eyes staring listlessly into the distance.

Don't talk to me about Kiely, Padraig had once said. *He's as lecherous a buck as ever pulled off his trousers. I don't know what the girls see in the skinny gudgeon; sure he looks half-witted with that cowlick above his ear.*

When Samuel joined Padraig, Padraig flicked a glance at the men, leaned toward Samuel, and switched to Spanish as they always did when discussing officers and topics that might get them into trouble.

"Someone cut the bow and stern lines. Halyards too, like I said. I know you don't want to believe one of ours would do that, but it's true. And I know you don't want to believe it was that bastard Maxwell either, but it was, I tell you. He wanted to drown me in last night's storm."

Samuel jammed his cold hands under his armpits and focused on the distant headland.

The cruel jibes of his classmates flashed through his mind— Papist lover, weakling, little almost lord. He'd always been afraid of his fellow Anglo-Irish in boarding school, especially the aristocrats. Boys like Maxwell. The thought of crossing them still made him queasy.

"You're imagining it. What do you think, that he was signaling the Russians? That's insane. He's a peer of the realm and hails from an impeccable family."

"I told you what I saw. Who cares if he's a bloody lord? They're all bastards, and you should know. That duel with that wretch, Greenfell, wasn't warning enough?"

Samuel sighed. He'd buried memories of that ill-fated day deep in the vault of his mind, grateful that nobody had died. He had been but a boy, only fifteen. Too young to be dueling over anything, yet Greenfell, a grown man, had forced him into it when Samuel had tried to stop him from murdering a starving tenant that Greenfell's thugs were evicting.

"You saved me that time for certain, and I shouldn't dismiss your concern today. Sorry, I should have told William. It's just—"

"Forget it. Let's focus on getting back to the regiment now." Padraig lifted his hands from the tiller and blew on them. "Worry about slipping us past sixty thousand Russians, them and their hairy-arsed Cossacks."

Adam Price sat up and pointed. "Look at all the smoke."

A dozen columns of smoke smeared the distant landscape, smudging the brightening sky.

Samuel threw up an arm to shade his eyes. "The Russians must be burning everything before we march, like they did against Napoleon. Either that or they're using the invasion to exterminate the Tartars."

"Oh, so you were paying attention to my lectures then," Padraig said with his cheeky grin.

"Only to filter out the lies." He wasn't giving Padraig any credit; it would only make his head bigger.

"The Russians want to wipe them out because they're Muslims." Padraig pointed to a rope attached to the sail. "Price, tighten up on that sheet. The rope, you Liverpool clown, and you looking for the sheet your mammy put on your bed."

The sky brightened as Padraig coaxed the ungainly raft toward the coast through a calming sea, and Samuel ordered the men to load their Colts. Thanks to General Brudenell's influence and money, the Light Brigade had received the first of the new six-shot Navy Colt revolvers delivered to the Queen's forces back in March. They'd practiced with the revolvers in Bulgaria and found them far superior to the muzzle-loaded single-shot pistols carried by most of the army. The Russians would have no gun to match them. The Colt's seven-and-a-half-inch octagonal barrel—in a weapon with an overall length of fourteen inches— made it highly portable for cavalry, and Samuel had drilled his men to cock the hammer and fire the single-action revolvers with either hand to keep their dominant hands free to wield a saber.

The shoreline grew more distinct—jagged gullies and rocky outcroppings resolving from the blur of brown land—as Padraig steered them in.

Samuel moved to the center of the raft. "Pay attention, men. Price, you too. We don't know who's watching, so let's get the horses ashore quickly. Sergeant Major, you and Kiely will climb to high ground and keep watch while we work. Questions?"

"Yes, sir," Hoffman said. "Any chance we can have a drink? Kiely's hogging all the water for the horses."

It was always Hoffman. "You can hold on a little longer. The horses are vital. We must do all we can for them since we need them to take us back."

"Not like you, Hoffman," Price said. "You're useless baggage, and we should toss you overboard now. We're seven with only six horses, and that way I'll have your horse."

"That's enough. Price, you can ride double behind Begley; you're both light." Samuel pointed to the haversacks. "They kept the powder dry so far, but let's not push our luck. As we beach, form a chain and pass the bags ashore, always holding them high above your heads."

Three hours later the raft surfed onto a rocky beach south of the headland, and Kiely and Wagner climbed the sandy bluff to keep watch as the others struggled in the surf to unload the supplies and horses. When they finished, Padraig headed out to check the immediate area for signs of the enemy.

Samuel's feet were freezing by the time they had coaxed the horses up to the wild grass on the bluff, and the blistering sun was welcome when he sat down to his ration of bread and peas; they dared not light a fire. He removed the oilskin cloth protecting his carbine and loaded it. Colonel Lawrence would have had a fit if he saw that weapon. *Not regulation. Not regulation at all, Kingston,* he'd whine in his nasally voice. *Get rid of it or I'll break you down to a cornet.*

While most cavalrymen still hankered after a glorious charge, Samuel believed those days were over. In today's battles, artillery and rifles could stop any such assault. The new role of the cavalry was to move into position quickly and strike hard, and a carbine was the perfect tool for a cavalryman. He'd ordered the carbine in London before shipping out and fallen in love with it.

"Do you know where we are, sir?"

Samuel swallowed his last bite of hard bread and lifted his head.

Prussian-born Sergeant Major Wagner was the hard-baked professional who'd run the company since before Samuel joined the regiment.

"More or less. We're on the south side of the Alma River, I believe, and that means we've about twenty-five miles to go before we get back to the regiment."

Wagner continued packing his pipe. "Do you think the navy's looking for us, Captain?"

With cholera killing hundreds of troops, it was doubtful the navy would spare the men to search for them. "Even if they did, we can't be sure they'll find us. We're better off pushing on."

Wagner was examining a box of matches. "Dry, thank God. I'm dying for a smoke. Twenty-five miles . . . It could be worse, sir. But we need to rest the horses. They're shagged."

"We'll hole up somewhere today, and tonight we'll m—"

Padraig crested the hill and then scrambled down. Samuel knew that look on his face.

"Arm yourselves, boys; something's wrong." He sprang to his feet and strode to meet Padraig.

"Cossacks!" Padraig called out. "They're raiding a farm; I heard a woman screaming." He stopped, rested his hands on his thighs, and panted.

A tic fluttered beneath Samuel's left eye, and he jammed a fist against it, determined to stop it. "How many?"

"I counted six. Hairy bastards are robbing the place and raping a girl."

Six. They could manage that number, and they needed intelligence. "Begley, stay here with the horses. Rest of you, pistols and sabers; we attack on foot."

Wagner blew out a plume of smoke, and the aromatic smell of tobacco reminded Samuel of his father. Too quickly the wind snatched away both scent and a sense of peace. The serenity of Springbough Manor was a world away from this hostile beach, but by golly, he'd make it back there some day, and no Cossack would stop him.

"Why would you risk that, sir?" Wagner tamped the pipe's bowl with a fat finger. "We should slip past them or wait them out. Buggers will move on once they've had their fun."

"What if they don't?" Samuel slung his carbine over his shoulder. He'd only twenty rounds for it, and he'd have to husband them. "What if they come this way next? Besides, we need a prisoner to tell us where the enemy's deployed."

"We can't slip by them, Sergeant Major," Padraig said. "The cottage sits beside the only path out of here. The land's flat; they'd see us if we were a mile away."

"That settles it," Samuel said. "We need to get through tonight; seven mounted men in uniform will be spotted in daylight tomorrow for certain." He didn't add that he'd never tolerate rape; that personal stand wasn't a professional excuse to make a ruckus behind enemy lines.

His homemade sling worked well, so snug a fit that he didn't even feel the carbine on his back as he climbed the loamy hill. The smell of vegetation was strong after the absence of such odors at sea as Padraig led them three hundred yards through wild grass. They crouched behind a briar ditch. Shouts and hammering came from the other side. Peering through the brambles, Samuel counted six horses grazing outside a wooden shack. There was no sign of the riders, but several red lances lay on the ground. Samuel placed his chapka in the dirt and drew his saber; the worn leather on the hilt was comforting and familiar. He nodded to Wagner, and the stout sergeant major tiptoed away with Price and Hoffman to circle behind the cottage.

Not five minutes later Wagner bobbed up behind a clump of bushes and signaled—they were ready. Drawing his saber with his right hand, Samuel filled his left hand with his Colt and nodded to Padraig and Kiely. All three sprinted to the open window, and heart pounding, Samuel crouched to listen. The harsh chatter of drunk men spilled out together with a soft mewling sound. He peeked through the window, and the stink of sweat, oily wool, and wine slammed through him.

Two men in gray greatcoats and black fur hats had pinned a girl spread-eagled on the table, and the clothes torn from her skinny body littered the earthen floor beside a prone peasant.

Blood trickled from a wound in her scalp, and the girl's white nakedness shocked Samuel. Animals. One of the Cossacks grunted as he dropped his trousers in front of the girl, and three more Cossacks jeered behind him.

Six. They were all there. Bastards. He beckoned to Padraig and Kiely and made a show of holstering his gun. They would do this silently. When he pointed at the door, they darted forward and met him there.

He burst through the open doorway, and a bearded Cossack turned toward him. The back door crashed open and Wagner charged in, followed by Hoffman and Price. Samuel slashed the bearded Cossack's throat with his saber, and warm blood spurted over his hand, drops tasting like iron salt on his lips. He shouldered the man beside him with his full weight, driving him to the floor, and Padraig skewered him where he fell. The girl's attacker's face screwed up, his eyes bulging, when Wagner smashed him on the head with the hilt of his saber. He collapsed in a tangle with his trousers around his ankles. Price swung his saber with a curse, and the men holding the girl's arms hollered and collapsed. Behind them, Price's face was twisted in fury as he pulled back his blade, and blood splashed Hoffman as Hoffman stepped back from his kill. Samuel's men were hard men, simple men, but for them, rape was beyond the pale.

Samuel spun, checking that there were no more of them, and Price stabbed the unconscious Cossack with a roar, bouncing from foot to foot as if he'd lost his mind. He was a savage bastard at the best of times, but Samuel understood exactly what he was feeling.

The Cossacks were down, all dead.

"Corporal, find something to cover the girl, for God's sake. Kiely, see to the man on the floor. Is he dead?"

Kiely, pallid and quaking, stood unmoving. It was a lot of

slaughter for a young mind to take, and poor Kiely was more squeamish than the others. *Kiely's a lover, not a fighter*, Padraig had once said, *but he'll not let us down*.

"Sergeant Major, check that man." Samuel touched the girl's head gently, but she recoiled with a scream. "Sorry, sorry, we mean you no harm." Fool; she couldn't understand him. None of them could. His plan hadn't considered that.

"He's alive. Looks like they bashed him on the head." Wagner was still breathless.

Blood covered the floor, seeping into the dirt, its copper smell mingling with the stench of piss and shit. Samuel's stomach churned.

Padraig placed a ragged blanket over the girl, but she whimpered and cringed.

"Find water quickly," Samuel told him. Samuel crouched beside the gray-bearded man. "Trooper Kiely, get a hold of yourself and take picket duty with Hoffman. Sergeant Major, fetch Begley and the horses and secure the Cossacks' horses as well; we can ride them and give our horses a chance to recover."

The peasant moaned and stirred. He looked old, a narrow fellow with a sallow complexion, receding black hair, and thin colorless lips. His dark eyes were unfocused when they opened, and he babbled in a guttural language Samuel took to be Russian.

"Easy now, we're British." Samuel forced what he hoped was a softer face and held up his empty hands for the man to see.

The peasant's dark eyes sharpened, and he spoke in Russian again.

With no clue what the man was saying, Samuel shook his head.

Pinching his lips together, the peasant propped up on his elbows. "Fr-Français?"

Samuel brightened. The only useful skill he'd picked up in boarding school had been French, and as he'd spoken Spanish all his life, French had come easily. "Yes, I speak French. Why did the Cossacks attack you?" He accepted a chipped mug from Price and held it to the man's lips.

The man gulped down the water and spluttered. Eventually he said, "You're French?"

"British."

"We're Tartars. When we heard the army had landed, many of us rebelled to join them, hoping to end our oppression." The peasant spoke French with the queer formality of a man unused to speaking the language. "I snuck down to the river and made notes of the Russian positions, intending to deliver them to the invading forces, but somebody betrayed me. Cursed Crimea . . . Full of rats who'd betray you for the price of a goat."

"It's the same in Ireland, too many traitors. Your notes, you still have them?"

The Tartar pushed into a sitting position, and his eyes welled with tears. "Taliba, my daughter. Is she—"

"Easy now, she's unharmed; we arrived in time." And the men had been more interested in slaking their thirst first, no doubt believing that had plenty of time to hurt the girl. Samuel helped the man off the floor. He was gaunt and featherlight.

The Tartar plucked the girl from the table and took her into his arms, speaking to her in Russian. Taliba threw her arms around her father and whimpered into his neck. She was young, perhaps sixteen, with an oval face and dark eyes darting like a trapped mouse. Even the blood and grime marring her golden skin couldn't hide her beauty. She clung to her father and peered at Samuel with bulging eyes.

Samuel bent to wipe his saber on the trousers of the dead Cossack at his feet. "We can't stay here; there might be more of them about. Your notes, where are they? Did the Cossacks take them? What's your name? I'm Lieutenant Kingston."

When the man straightened, he was almost Padraig's height. "My name's Giray, and I'm too smart for those sheep shaggers; I hid my notes well. Do you want to see them?"

"Damned right, I do."

Giray had notes all right, tattered pages filled with penciled handwriting, troop counts, and even a rough map. And everything was legible—if one read Russian.

Padraig's fair face was ruddy from the sea and the exertion as he crowded Samuel at the table. "What did he say? What's that, a map?"

"Yes, a map. Now shut up and let me talk to him." Samuel's pulse quickened when he recognized Calamita Bay. "Is that smudged line the Alma River?"

Giray bobbed his head and pointed to a shaded area next to the river. "The heights. The Russians have built . . . How do you say . . . like walls for guns? Made of mud. No, earth. Do you understand?"

"Redoubts," Samuel guessed.

"Yes. Two of them. And I counted one hundred big, big guns."

"Artillery," Samuel suggested. "One hundred pieces in total?" Samuel's skin tingled. Enough cannons to destroy the allied advance.

Giray nodded.

"This number here—forty thousand—is that your total troop count?" Samuel stabbed his finger at the notepaper.

"It's estimate, but close."

"Forty thousand," Samuel said slowly, and Giray nodded and repeated the number.

Samuel translated for Padraig. Padraig was no officer, but he'd read more military books than any officer in the Seventeenth. One wall of shelves was full of them in the library at Springbough Manor. Samuel trusted his mind and his quick read of a tactical situation.

Turning away, Padraig covered his mouth. "The hills behind the Alma. Good Lord, our infantry will have to wade through the river and climb those hills while that bloody artillery batters them every step of the way."

"What about the coast side?" Samuel asked Giray. "Why no

guns on that flank?"

Giray smiled unexpectedly. "They must believe the cliffs too steep to scale, but they are wrong. As boys, my friends and I often climbed those cliffs in search of wild birds' eggs."

Samuel tapped a stack of pages. Now that could be an opportunity. The allies, with sixty-five thousand troops, outnumbered the Russians. But Samuel knew that the Russian numbers were actually greater. Which meant that General Menshikov must believe himself well defended if he'd leave the rest of his army behind the fortifications of Sevastopol. "Can you show me the redoubts and other defenses?"

"No!" Giray waved both hands. "It's too dangerous; they might see you."

"We can wear the Cossacks' greatcoats." Spying on the enemy from this side of their defenses was too great an opportunity to miss.

Hoofbeats sounded beyond the open window.

The others had brought the horses. Samuel looked at Price as Giray plucked on his dry bottom lip. "Price, help the lads search for fodder and feed the horses." He turned back to Giray. "We just saved your lives; you owe us."

Giray hesitated before saying, "Perhaps tonight."

That would be too late. They needed darkness to sneak past the Russians. The allies, impatient after the time lost in the disastrous landing, might be advancing already.

Samuel updated Padraig.

"What if they march in the morning against those monstrous guns?" Padraig asked.

"Exactly. We must move now. We can't return without this information; it could save hundreds of lives. You and I will go with him. We'll wear the Cossacks' coats and hats. Giray, is there somewhere along the way the others can hide and wait?"

"We can leave them at the edge of the forest, two miles from here," Giray said.

He was putting himself and Padraig at greater risk, but he

had to take the chance. If all went well, they'd rejoin the others before nightfall. And if not . . . Wagner would have to lead the men back alone.

———

The rain returned and lashed them that afternoon when Samuel, Padraig, and Giray trotted out of the rolling grassland. It reminded Samuel of the Black Water Valley back in Ireland, but it had few signs of habitation. Only the last gasps of smoke from a handful of burned-out farms, proof the Russians were attacking the Tartars, and a few stands of trees broke the monotony of the endless grasses.

So this was the beginning of the desolate steppes stretching into Ukraine that he'd seen on the map.

Giray wore a Cossack greatcoat over his smock and looked like one of them as he rode beside Samuel—save for the bloody saber slash on the back of the coat. They had left the lancers with Taliba in a forest three miles back. The stiff wind smelled of rain and smoke but wasn't potent enough to sweep away the malodor of stale sweat and damp wool steaming from Samuel's greatcoat.

He took off the soggy fur hat and scratched his head. The hat and coat crawled with lice, and they were biting him all over. He sought a distraction.

"How did you learn to speak French, Giray?"

"I traveled with my master to trade in Constantinople, where he had much business with the French." Giray's flat eyes tightened. "The Russians murdered him three years ago. Now I'm left with nothing."

Wailing and shrieks sounded in the distance, and Samuel drew his Colt as three smoking log huts materialized from the haze, ramshackle buildings with low doorways better suited as doghouses. A handful of men, women, and children dressed in

ragged smocks with their feet wrapped in dirty bandages staggered among bodies strewn across the ground.

Samuel straightened in his saddle. "Bloody hell."

"Serfs," Giray said calmly, as if ragged people walking among
the dead were an everyday occurrence. "They likely resisted
when the Cossacks ransacked the place. The poor wretches have
no food to feed an army, yours or the Russians'. They had
cabbage and lard soup if they were lucky, nettles if they were not.
Now they have nothing."

"But how can the Russians get away with that?" Samuel
looked away from a gaunt woman. "Why's that woman wearing
an iron collar?"

"These people are serfs. Slaves. Their master can whip them,
send them to Siberia, even kill them if he wishes."

How could any humans be so cruel? Samuel's lips curled. But
sometimes it was as bad in Ireland. Not the collar—that was
barbaric—but landowners treated their peasants as they pleased,
and it had been far worse six years ago during the famine, when
they had starved tenants, evicted them, and even murdered
them. He remembered William Greenfell and frowned. Well,
that bugger was walking Clonakilty with a limp now, *and* his
name was a disgrace because he'd cheated in the duel.

When the serfs spotted them, they staggered into flight.

"Why are their feet wrapped in ragged bandages?" Padraig
asked.

Samuel translated the question.

"Not bandages, puttees—long strips of cloth to protect their
legs and keep them warm." Giray's half-hearted shrug, his indifference, spoke volumes about the cruelty in that harsh land.

Samuel couldn't bear to see more, and he nudged the Cossack
gelding with his heels. "Come along," he said. "The Cossacks
may still be about."

They rode on in silence, but Samuel couldn't get the serfs out
of his mind. Russia was like Ireland, only worse. Irish peasants
had few rights, but Russians apparently had none at all. In his

English boarding school, professors had spoken of how Russians abused the serfs, but never of how the British mistreated the Irish. The plight of the serfs was even worse than they'd said, but then again, so was the abuse of the Irish. When he returned home, he'd join father's crusade to improve conditions for the Catholics. He stared ahead bleakly. If he ever returned.

Padraig dipped the lance in his hand and made a face. "I don't see why we brought these pig-stickers; they're not even well-balanced."

Just like his father, who'd served as a sergeant major in the Royal Irish Dragoons during the Peninsular Wars and later drilled the boys with weapons from the time they were old enough to pick up a stick, Padraig preferred to fight with his saber.

Samuel, who favored the power and range of newer weapons, said, "It's part of the disguise. If you wanted to use your saber, perhaps we should have murdered a few hussars."

"Don't you worry," Padraig said. "There's time for that yet. Though I'd prefer to kill a Cossack and take one of those weird sabers as a souvenir. A shashka they call it. Pity the buggers back there had none. They must have been pauper Cossacks."

"The sabers without a proper guard, you mean." Samuel dragged his fetid sleeve across his eyes to clear the rain away.

"That's the one." Padraig reached inside his coat and scratched his chest. "Bloody lice. The shashka has a guard, but it's little more than a lip. So when you fight the buggers, try to slice their fingers off."

"I hope we won't fight at all," Samuel said. "We'll hang well back out of sight, reconnoiter the Russian defenses, and dash back to the lads."

Once they reached the end of the flatland, they found themselves on one of the two hills overlooking the coastal road from Eupatoria to Sevastopol.

Giray reined in. "They are below us."

Samuel glassed the two earthwork fortifications squatting

halfway down the forward slope of the heights. Below the earthworks, the Russians had cleared the area all the way to the river's red banks to create a killing ground, and thousands of infantrymen lounged behind the ramparts. Europe hadn't seen a sight like it since Bonaparte's aggression forty years before.

Samuel turned his spyglass to the coast but couldn't make out the cliffs. "Are you sure you climbed those cliffs?"

"Many times," Giray said. "Have you seen what you needed to see? Can we go back now?" He eyed the trail behind them and bit his lip. "I remind you that you promised to take Taliba and me with you to the allied camp."

Sure, it would be so easy. All they had to do was ride past forty thousand Russians and charge their pickets. Samuel broke eye contact with the Tartar. "That was our deal. I've seen enough. Let's go." He reached under his coat and felt the Colt. It was still dry, snug in its holster. He'd left the carbine with the others; it would have been hard to keep a dry charge in it.

Their Cossack ponies may have been small, but they were spirited, and Samuel pushed them hard, eager to rejoin the others and move on.

When the forest materialized out of the rain after forty minutes, he lifted up a silent prayer of thanks.

Hooves drummed the turf on their left, and his heart started racing when a dozen horsemen, sabers waving, galloped out of a dip in the ground a hundred yards away, yelling as they sprang their trap.

Samuel spurred his lathered horse and cried out, "To the woods. Ride!"

Giray whimpered and jerked his reins wildly in his panic, sending his horse crashing into Samuel's.

Samuel kicked off his stirrups as he was thrown, but he landed hard, banging his skull and huffing the wind from his chest. Pain seared through him, and pinpoints of light flashed before his eyes. He struggled to his feet on what felt like shifting ground.

Padraig had reined in and drawn his Colt, but Giray lay in the mud.

Whooping and yelling, the Cossacks with lances couched them at the gallop. They were going to ride them down. Samuel palmed his Colt.

The Cossacks slewed their mounts to a halt five yards away, spraying him with mud. That was when Samuel spotted the hussar in blue, a black shako perched tall upon his head. A man as pale and blond as the Cossacks were dark and weathered.

Though the Cossacks outnumbered them, the six-shot Colts somewhat evened the odds, but when the lead flew and lances stabbed, Samuel and Padraig would die. Samuel clutched the Colt hard to steady his trembling hand.

The officer hadn't drawn a weapon. And now he sat back in the saddle, lit a cheroot, and fixed Samuel with one icy-blue eye while the other, a lazy eye, looked toward the steppes.

"I've been searching for you castaways. You've been murdering Russians . . ." He negligently waved his cheroot. "Colonel Peter Orlov at your service. I promise you spies a fair trial if you come quietly."

His French was impeccable, delivered with a clipped voice that grated like glass.

Samuel stepped into a wide stance. "We're not spies. We were washed away from the fleet, and we're trying to return to the bay."

Orlov raised his chin and blew a stream of smoke into the air. "You're out of uniform—that makes you spies. Why did you murder my soldiers?"

Before Samuel could answer—he had no answer ready— hoofbeats sounded and five lancers broke from the forest one hundred yards away, red and white pennants flapping on their upright lances. The Cossacks looked that direction instinctively, and Samuel opened fire. The revolver kicked, spurting smoke, and the Cossack closest to Orlov folded over his saddle with a grunt. Thumbing back the hammer, Samuel fired at Orlov, but missed. Another Cossack was already racing toward him, and Samuel jumped clear of the lance even as a bullet knocked off Samuel's chapka. His third shot hit the Cossack's horse, and it stampeded away. He kept firing at the riders, Padraig's Colt barking beside him, and tasted brimstone as smoke billowed back on him.

Four Cossacks tumbled from their saddles as the lancers thundered close. Suddenly the remaining Cossacks dropped back and wheeled away. His head pounding, Samuel aimed at a fleeing rider and pulled the trigger, but the hammer dropped with a mechanical click.

Empty.

The gunfire died, and six Cossacks lay in the meadow where four horses whinnied pitifully, thrashing about on the trampled grass. Colonel Orlov was galloping east with the rest of his men, toward the Russian positions above the Alma.

What of his own men? Samuel spun around. Padraig was crouched over his Colt, sheltering it from the rain as he reloaded, and the other five were still mounted, faces streaked with rain-washed black powder, and all, even Wagner, grinning like fools.

Samuel laughed shakily. "What kept you?" But it was hard to present a brave front when forty thousand Russians stood between them and the allied army. And when he knew that the allies faced hell between those two Russian redoubts. He resisted the weariness that dragged at his bones.

The enemy knew they were there and were searching for them.

It was imperative to warn the allies before Orlov silenced him and his men permanently.

CHAPTER THREE

September 18, 1854

Orlov and his Cossacks would return, so therefore the lancers must do the unexpected. Samuel led his weary band from the forest after dark and took Giray's advice to ride west and use a ravine near the coast to slip past the Russian lines.

He'd been tempted to wear the Cossack greatcoat against the biting cold but ultimately chose not to. He still itched all over, and the thought of sharing it with Russian flees curled his toes. While Goldie hadn't recovered her golden luster, the palomino had a bounce in her step as she picked her way through the tall grass. Earlier, after reloading their weapons, Samuel had stood guard while his men and the horses had snatched a miserable rest in the rain-soaked woods.

They'd been lucky in that skirmish. Wagner's attack had surprised the Russians, who'd failed to injure a single lancer. With guns like the Colts, war would never be the same again. Even Giray appeared none the worse for his injury. But the Cossacks would return with reinforcements and likely scour the countryside for them. Samuel didn't like to rely on anyone, but

only Giray's knowledge of the terrain could keep them ahead of
their pursuers. Giray planned to stick to the forests and off the
main trail as much as possible.

"These Colts are incredible," Hoffman said behind Samuel.
"They made all the difference. We fired as much lead as a full
company of troopers."

"Yes, Hoffman," Kiely piped up. "That's the Queen's plan.
Guns that fire more bullets so she won't have to depend on your
scrawny ass. She'll kick you out of the regiment, and you'll have
to go back to poaching rabbits."

The clouds parted, and the half-moon was bright enough to
light the way. Samuel resisted the urge to make haste—if one
horse went lame, they would be in trouble. They hadn't brought
the extra mounts after all. Slipping nine riders through the
Russian lines would be tough enough. They didn't need to
stretch the train with extra horses.

Heading for the broken ground at the coast south of the
Alma River, they traversed the grassland in two ranks. Giray
rode beside Samuel, and save for the bump like a pigeon's egg on
his forehead, he'd recovered from his fall. Padraig trotted on
Samuel's right, chattering to Taliba though she couldn't understand a word he said. She'd perked up after her ordeal in the
cabin, and her intelligent eyes swept the grassland constantly.
Samuel twisted in the saddle to check the others.

Begley had changed position in the second line again and was
now watching Hoffman's chestnut. A farm boy from the
Midlands, he was better than the regiment's veterinary officer,
constantly checking the horses. He always knew when a beast
was out of sorts. Hoffman was twisting his stringy hair around
his fingers and humming tunelessly. Price was glaring in every
direction, seeming to despise Crimea as much as he did the rest
of the world. Squat, with close-cropped brown hair, a high forehead, and a nose broken in two places, he looked like a bulldog
and behaved like one too. The oldest man in C Company—
Samuel guessed he was forty—Price had grown up in the slums

of Liverpool and was always spoiling for a fight. Russian, French, or British, he didn't care who he tangled with, but when it came to a fight, he was loyal to the company. That said, all Samuel's men were solid, and that might be just enough to get them back to the regiment.

Kiely, the youngster, was cocking a leg and testing the girth of his saddle again; he had done it at least ten times already, a sure sign of nerves, though nerves didn't stop him from ogling Taliba.

The sergeant major stole another drink from the silver flask slipped from his tunic. All were gaunt and pale from living in that squalid camp in Bulgaria and from eating only rotting salt meat and spoiled vegetables, but men like them were the heart of the British army and tough as oak. Though regulations forbade him from even shaking their hands, he cared about every one of them. He'd get them back to the safety of the regiment or die in the effort. The rest of the regiment probably thought their missing comrades had drowned, and poor William would agonize over the letter he'd write to Father. Well, they were all in for a surprise, them and Maxwell. Samuel ground his teeth. That weasel had much to explain.

"Isn't she a beauty, Hoffman?" Kiely asked none too quietly as they passed through a small wood with moonlight bright on the broken ground beyond. "I'm in love with her dark eyes, how they blazed in the sunlight earlier."

Hoffman scratched the scar over his left eye—Padraig told Samuel he'd heard that a whore had smacked him with a bottle back in Hounslow. "Who are you yapping about?"

"The Indian girl." Kiely's voice thickened. "I'm in love. Do you think we could bring her back to England?"

Hoffman grunted. "She's not an Indian, you brainless woebegone. She's a tartan."

"Oh. You mean like a Highlander? That's all right, I love her anyway. Look at her hair. It's as silky as a mare's—"

Padraig chuckled. "She's a Tartar, not a tartan, and definitely no Indian, you fool. Just shut your gob, Kiely. You're not going anywhere near that poor girl. One sniff of you, and she'll run back to the Cossacks."

"But, Corporal, I'm just telling you what's in my heart."

"Next time tell us what's in your head," Padraig said. "That'll take no time at all. Now shut your hole and watch the skyline, or 'tis a Cossack you'll be dancing with."

The banter was good for morale, but Padraig knew how to check it and keep the men alert.

The lancers sniggered, and Giray looked over at Samuel, raising his hands.

"A stupid joke that doesn't translate." Samuel patted Goldie's silver mane and hid his smile. "How much farther?"

Giray pushed the hair from his eyes, wincing when he touched the bump on his head. "An hour, perhaps. I hope I can find the ravine and pray the Russians are not guarding it."

"Let's get there first, then we c—"

Four men rose from the tall grass fifteen feet ahead, brandishing muskets and calling out in Russian.

Samuel flinched, and his hand flew to the flap of his holster. Bloody hell, not again.

Three more ambushers rose from the grass on the right, and another two on Samuel's left, shadowy men in dark smocks wearing fur caps with long flaps.

"Don't," Giray squeaked. "Bandits. There'll be more of them."

"Hands off your weapons, boys." Samuel stretched out a hand to still Padraig beside him. "There's more of them."

Almost immediately riders thundered out of the trees and hauled up like a rearing wave in front of the lancers, brandishing swords and pistols. Samuel clenched his jaw. What a fool he was; he should have had scouts out. He slowly withdrew his hand from his holster. He was so damned tired, he hadn't been thinking straight "Bandits?"

Giray was quaking in the saddle. "I th-th-think so."

A giant of a man with unkempt black hair dangling from under his fur cap dismounted with surprising agility and lumbered up to Giray, booming something unintelligible. Giray's lips moved, but no words came at first. Samuel edged Goldie closer to Giray. He couldn't do much to protect him, though. Not while staring down the barrel of a musket.

When Giray finally spoke, his voice was shrill and halting. The big man laughed—a deep, intimidating rumble—and his voice boomed again. His head was square, overlarge even for his enormous body, and after a quick survey, Samuel realized his bulky fur cloak exaggerated his size.

"His name is Hamza Sharipov." Giray's voice trembled. "He says he's a Tartar tribal leader. He and his men were on their way to join the British liberators when their scout spotted us. They presumed we were Russians and planned to attack us."

Samuel's muscles relaxed. What good fortune, allies . . . The Tartars might know of a way to pass the Russian lines. Those of Sharipov's men on foot moved closer and began petting the horses, fingering the saddles like shoppers in a marketplace, and squinting at the lancers' weapons. The sixteen men—Samuel realized he could call them rebels—were dressed in the loose smocks and puttees worn by serfs.

"They may still murder us," Giray continued. "I've heard of this man . . . He *is* a bandit. And notorious in these parts."

Sharipov strode right up to Goldie and petted her nose. Goldie threw up her head with a whinny and sidestepped. He laughed, thrust his hands to his hips—his arms were as big as Samuel's thighs—and spoke again, his voice as loud as a horn. The stink of his breath—like rotting meat—churned Samuel's gut, and when he angled his head toward Giray, Samuel saw that the Tartar's face had drained to white.

Giray blinked rapidly and spoke again. "He says your palomino's the finest horse he's ever seen, perfect for breeding, and now that you are allies, you should gift her to him."

A horse reared behind Samuel, and Price swore. "Get your paws off my holster, you hairy-arsed prick."

Pressure pulsed in Samuel's head. They wouldn't be able to talk their way out of this. "Count of three, my lads, go for your guns." He smiled at Sharipov, forced a laugh, and nodded his acquiescence.

Sharipov must have been confident in his superior numbers, because a crack appeared in his bushy beard, exposing four or five black teeth.

"One," Samuel called cheerfully, beaming at Sharipov. The crook was confident, yes, but the bastard had never seen a Navy Colt. "Two." Samuel bent forward as if to dismount.

He had always had fast hands, and for five years he'd practiced drawing and firing with both hands—adding the left because he needed his right to wield his saber.

"Three!" Samuel whipped out the Colt, thumbing back the hammer as he swung it to bear on Sharipov, who had a massive head he couldn't miss.

The Colt blazed, blinding in the darkness, and Sharipov's head whipped back. Guns cracked all around Samuel, the barks of the Colts sharper than the flat reports of the bandits' ancient pistols and muskets. Goldie lunged into the pack of riders and bit deep into one horse's shoulder as Samuel fired, point-blank, at the rider. The bandit's screech cut off abruptly, and the man collapsed. Samuel cocked and shot as fast as he could, swinging his Colt from one bandit to the next, assured his men would deal with the bandits on foot. His desperate cry chorused with the shouts of "death or glory" and the screams of the wounded as he counted every shot.

. . . six. He flipped the revolver to his left hand and drew his saber. "Kill them all." They couldn't risk leaving one man alive to betray them to the Russians.

Jerry Kerr had trained Goldie well, and unbidden she carried Samuel to the last two mounted bandits. A snarling gray-mustached man swung his shashka wildly, and a shock shot up

Samuel's arm as he blocked the strike and sliced down the bandit's blade to cut off his fingers. The bandit screeched, and Samuel rammed his blade into his chest, feeling it grate against ribs. The second bandit's shashka flashed down, and Samuel touched Goldie with his toe. She whirled left around the attacker, allowing Samuel to swing backhanded and cut deep into the man's neck. Blood spurted over his hand, warm and sticky, and Samuel gave an exultant cheer, surprised he was still alive.

The bandits' loose horses whinnied around him before bolting north. A shadow vaulted from the ground and mounted a horse as it took off, clinging to it like a barnacle.

"*Schwein!*" Moonlight flashed on Wagner's lance as he couched it and spurred his mount past Samuel. "I'll get the bastard."

Price, on foot, screamed as his saber rose and fell like a farmer scything corn. "All right, ye bastards, ye know the routine." *Thud, thud.* "Take this from the Queen . . . and this . . . and *this*."

"Death or glory!" Wagner rose in the stirrups and punched his lance into the fleeing bandit's back with a wet-sounding *slap*, driving it deep. The man screeched, and the horse pitched over as Wagner rode past, trailing his hand to pull the bloody lance free from the falling bodies. "That'll teach you to rob the Seventeenth."

Breathless, Samuel wheeled Goldie left and right, and she pranced handsomely, her war blood up as the regiment's war cry stirred his own blood.

When the last bandit fell, he swung down from the saddle and ran from bloody body to bloody body; all were dead. The wounded horses writhed on the blood-soaked grass, their screams twisting his insides. He stabbed his bloody saber into the ground and instinctively rummaged in the cartridge box slung from his shoulder as he counted his men.

Wagner was spearing a fallen bandit; Price was doubled over and panting; Padraig stood at the edge of the battleground, looking north; and Hoffman and Giray crouched over a body. Cold rippled down Samuel's spine, and he raced toward them.

Before he reached them, Samuel swerved to a stop beside a kneeling Begley. He was pressing a bloody rag to Kiely's shoulder.

"Kiely, how bad as it?"

Kiely was ashen, breathing in shallow pants. "I . . . I—"

"Just winged 'im, sir," Begley croaked. "I'll patch 'im up, sir, I will. You hear me, Kiely, old mate?"

"Good lad, Begley. Hear that, Kiely? Begley's said you're going to be right as rain." Samuel pawed at the sweat stinging his eyes despite the bitter cold and hastened to Hoffman and Giray.

The firing had stopped, but the horses' screams filled the night. Samuel averted his gaze from the thrashing bodies; he couldn't stand to watch or listen. He reached Hoffman and froze; Taliba lay between Hoffman and Giray, her innocent face blown off. His legs turned to jelly, and he fell to his knees beside them. He'd seen too much death on battlefields in his brief life, but never an innocent girl like Taliba. Never close up, and never an innocent he knew.

Begley dressed Kiely's wound while Giray cleansed Taliba's body with water from a nearby stream, and the rest of the lancers dug a shallow grave. Hoffman rinsed the smocks from three bandits in the stream so Giray could use them as a shroud, and they laid the body on its right side with the head facing toward Mecca. Giray's face was slack, his eyes vacant, as he muttered quick prayers, and when Samuel couldn't look at his sorrow any longer he tilted his face to the sky. Death was the reality of war. But no amount of glory was worth the lives of slaughtered innocents.

Each man threw three handfuls of dirt into the grave, and afterward they filled in the hole. The evening turned freezing cold after the hot day, and Samuel's belly churned as he helped Giray stack flat stones for a marker. Time was running out for the thousands of men who'd soon face the Russian forces gathered against them.

Within forty minutes of the last gunshot, they rode on, with a silent Giray slumped in the saddle, his dark eyes dull. Samuel's heart clenched at the Tartar's stoic acceptance of his only child's death. Crimea was a hard and brutal land, and they'd only just arrived.

He nudged Goldie alongside Giray and touched the Tartar's shoulder. "I'm sorry, Giray. Taliba didn't deserve this. You didn't. She was a wonderful girl."

Giray said nothing, just stared ahead.

Samuel feared that the brutality was just beginning. Even potential allies could be enemies, Cossacks hunted them, and thousands of Russians blocked their road home. He stopped his shoulders from slumping. He couldn't give up, no matter how tired he was, and he dare not make another mistake.

CHAPTER FOUR

September 18, 1854, evening

The cinder burns on the blue frock coat of his dress uniform appeared as big as a crater to Colonel Peter Orlov, and his blood boiled. It wasn't hard to use an iron; that damned serf was going to pay for his negligence. He snatched his shako from the cot and stormed from the tent into the freezing night. Two steps from the tent, one polished boot landed in a puddle and mud splatted his impeccable coveralls. Pressure surged in his head. Bastards. He'd ordered them to plank the path from his tent. The culprit who'd ignored him would rot in Siberia.

Below him, thousands of Russian campfires twinkled halfway down Kourgane Hill like a starlit belt. The reek of smoke, cabbage soup, and horse manure filled the early night's air. The Cossack sentries lowered their gazes as he marched past them to the blazing fire at the edge of the camp.

He didn't have time for this, not when that fool Denisov still hadn't captured the British lancers. Surely one hundred men were enough to throw a cordon above the heights.

Three Cossacks had stripped the serf to his waist and tied

him to a tree, and the wretch moaned and cringed as Orlov approached.

The bastard didn't even have the respect to take his punishment without shrinking away. Heat flushed Orlov's face, and he barreled forward. He'd teach the dog manners. He caught the whiff of vodka on the guard's breath as he snatched the nagaika from his hands. In almost the same moment, he lashed the serf's back. The serf screamed and sagged against the tree trunk.

"How dare you cringe from your punishment, pig? Don't you deserve this for failing me?" He twisted the whip's greasy handle in his hands. Thick, hardened leather, it would serve his purpose.

"Yes, F-Father. P-p-please correct me."

The serf attempted to straighten—a disgusting man with his ribs poking through, all skin and bones.

The scum had destroyed his best frock coat. Orlov's lips peeled back into a snarl, and he swung the nagaika with all his might, grunting with the effort. A rib caved, and the serf shrieked, sagging on the rope and panting. Orlov nodded curtly, stood wide, and punished the louse. Every lash of the short whip sent energizing shocks up his arm, making his blood race, and his breath came in rushed gasps. "You let me down. Nobody will ever do that again."

He flogged the serf over and over, though the wretch fell silent and his bleeding flesh was peeling from his bones. Power coursed through Orlov's veins. Warm, sticky blood dripped down his hands, fueling his fury. He smashed at the man until his arm was too weary to lift again and he was starved for breath. What a release it was to remind them of his domination.

He threw the bloody nagaika into the crimson-tinted quagmire a few yards beyond the tree. "Remove this offal from my camp. Let the wolves feed on him."

When hooves thundered up the gully, Orlov turned. His adjutant handed him a soft cloth, and he cleaned his hands. A guard challenged the newcomer, and someone replied.

The rhythmic wheeze of blown horses and the clink of

bridles sounded beyond the weak perimeter of firelight, and a horde of Cossacks galloped out of the darkness. The horses reared and pawed the air when their bearded riders hauled them up ten feet from Orlov.

Captain Denisov vaulted to the ground and bounded up to his commander. He was a narrow man, shorter than Orlov, with coal-black hair and a drooping mustache. "Colonel, I have a report of shots fired over by the coastal cliffs. Likely it's the British lancers."

"How? You told me they'd come this way. Why did you come back?" The man was a fool—did no one think for themselves? "Get back there and bring them in. The allies may march on the Alma in the morning, and those lancers must not get through to them."

Denisov cleared his throat. "Someone who knows the trails must be guiding them, sir. They've dodged our patrols."

Nobody had bested him before; he wanted every one of those cursed lancers dead. He should have pursued them himself, but Maxwell was coming. Well, the traitor's information had better be worth it. "You *loh*. And why did you return? Get back there and hunt the bastards."

"You ordered me to report, sir. I—"

A commotion broke out at the northern end of the camp, and somebody called out, "Let me through. I have an urgent message for the colonel."

A corporal sprinted into the firelight and waved a flighty salute, avoiding Orlov's eyes.

"Colonel, there's a British captain at the guard post. He has a pass from you and seeks an audience."

"Finally!"

About damned time. The prince was eager to know the strength of the allied forces. Information that Maxwell was keen to spill.

"Send him in. Denisov, take your men to the cliffs and bring me those lancers. Dead or alive, it's the same to me." He pulled

out his pocket watch. Seven p.m.; the prince must be frothing at
the mouth for news.

He glared into the campfire. What kind of man betrayed his
country? Worse, what kind of *aristocrat* betrayed his country?
True, Maxwell had Russian blood and was related to the army
commander, Prince Menshikov; the prince had revealed that
tidbit when he'd ordered Orlov to liaise with Maxwell. But half
the aristocrats in Europe married across their frontiers. As a
young woman, Queen Victoria once took a shine to Tsarevich
Alexander Nikolayevich himself, and the pair of them could have
married. But being family was no excuse for treason. Were that
the case, the world would be a muddle. He spat in the mud. To
hell with that.

Maxwell had the ruddy face of an Englishman, greasy hair
flowing down to his collar, a bald chin, and red pork chop sideburns. He didn't look trustworthy. He was of average height
when he dismounted from his charger, weight turning to the
heavy side. The toady probably fenced no longer, and as one of
General Airey's aides-de-camp, he'd never be in harm's way. But
Airey was Quartermaster-General of the British army, and *that*
gave the traitor access to Raglan's battle plans.

"It's a pleasure to meet you, sir." Maxwell held out a soft
hand. "All that mirror flashing . . . It's no way to have a
conversation."

Hearing the man speak, Orlov remembered an additional
detail. Menshikov had said that gambling debts had ruined
Maxwell, and that he was betraying his country for the promise
of estates in Russia. What a swine. Orlov ignored the proffered
hand.

"You're cutting it tight, sir. The prince is eager to know
Raglan's plans now, not when they're at the foot of our
ramparts."

Maxwell looked at his floating hand and swallowed. "I was
acting my role as scout and waiting for a chance to slip away. I
must be more careful. One officer suspected me. A wretch called

Kingston. I cut the raft with him and a handful of his lancers adrift in last night's storm. Hopefully, they drowned out at sea."

That was how they got there. Damn Maxwell for an incompetent idiot. "They didn't drown. I ran into them behind our lines this morning after they murdered my men, but they escaped. We've been scouring the area for them since."

Maxwell gasped. "Impossible. Nobody could have survived that gale."

"They did. We found their raft." This was a disaster. *Gandon.* Weakling. Maxwell was a spoiled aristocrat, but they needed him. It would be impossible to place another spy among Raglan's staff.

"You must catch them, Kingston and that snooping corporal of his." Maxwell's lips quivered. "If they make it back to our army, I'll face a noose."

Oh, he'd stop this Kingston all right. Not because he gave a damn about the soft Westerner, but because he couldn't afford to lose a valuable asset. Orlov bit back his anger. And because that brazen lieutenant had made a fool out of him that afternoon. "Do you have General Raglan's battle plan?"

"Where's Kingston now? You must cap—"

"The plans, sir. I must know Raglan's strategy; the future of the empire may depend on it."

"But that corporal saw me signal your men. I'll hang if—"

"To hell with them," Orlov snapped. "You should have been more careful." He grabbed Maxwell's tunic, and the Englishman's eyes popped open. "Do you have the information that I— That Prince Menshikov needs?" The bugger was the prince's cousin, so he'd better not rough him up. He loosened his fingers, and Maxwell recoiled.

"I do." Maxwell stooped and drew an oilskin package from one mud-spattered boot. "Tomorrow, the nineteenth of September, will go down in history as the day Mother Russia destroyed the combined armies of Britain, France, and the Ottoman Empire. It's all here." He waved the packet. "The

French, supported by the guns of the warships, will advance on the left flank beside the coast, and the British will march on the inland side of the Sevastopol road, with the Light Brigade guarding their flank. The landing at Calamita Bay was a disaster, and the Heavy Brigade has yet to finish disembarking. The Light Brigade will be the only cavalry in the field tomorrow."

Foul traitor, Orlov thought. "That'll be all. Return to Raglan's headquarters before you're missed." Orlov turned his back and hastened to his tent, the serf's blood drying to rust on his hands, his mind grinding.

Outside the tent, his adjutant, Lieutenant Galdin, leaped to his feet and saluted smartly. Short and corpulent, Galdin wasn't his type of soldier, but Orlov tolerated him as an efficient administrator.

He passed Maxwell's message to Galdin. "Make a copy." He'd keep the message for posterity and as proof that he masterminded the defeat of the allied army. "But first send for a messenger; I have an urgent message for General Menshikov."

Breathless, he ducked into his tent and snatched up a pencil. He'd recommend that Menshikov hide six thousand infantrymen in the low ground north of the river and use a squadron of Cossacks to tempt the Light Brigade into a trap. If they could eliminate the British cavalry tomorrow, a Russian victory was a foregone conclusion. The tsar himself would hear of this and honor him. The pencil stilled as he gazed into the distance and imagined the supreme ruler greeting him.

Imagined the great glory that might accompany such an honor.

CHAPTER FIVE

September 18, 1854, late evening

"You'd think this rain would drown these filthy Russian lice." Price was scratching inside the bloodstained greatcoat as they followed the cliffs north, searching for the ravine that Giray knew bypassed the Russian lines. "I don't think these Cossacks ever take a bath; they must be terrified of soap and water."

Begley was wringing water from his sheepskin hat. "How can they be afraid of a bath when pails of water spill from the sky every night?"

"If they're scared of soap and water, we're in luck," Hoffman said as another wave boomed at the foot of the cliffs far below. "Next time they jump us, we fire soap at them."

Price snorted. "Ha, Hoffy. You'll be the first to run if you even smell soap. I've never seen you bathe. You smell like my horse's arse."

"Shut your sauce box, Price." Sergeant Major Wagner spurred his mount up from behind and struck Price with the leather whip he'd taken from a dead Cossack. "Do you think you're old Bloodyback riding in Hyde Park with one of his doxies? There are thousands of Russians out there; you want to bring the bastards down on us?"

Samuel should chastise their irreverence, but they could all be dead by morning, so there was little point. Instead he hid his smile at the trooper's nickname for General Brudenell, a brute notorious for ordering men flogged for the slightest offense. They had only six Cossack uniforms, so he wore the bandit leader's sable cloak, hoping he could pass for an officer. Giray still wore his own ragged clothing, and with any luck a casual observer would believe he was a guide. Samuel groaned quietly. It was a weak plan, but all they had.

His eyes were gritty from lack of sleep and his body weary when Giray turned onto broken ground, rode on a hundred yards, and dismounted at a gully that descended steeply into the darkness. Rainwater gushed down the craggy walls and splashed into a gurgling stream.

Samuel drank water from his canteen and dismounted, and loose stones rattled underfoot. "Christ, it's steep. How deep is that stream?"

"Inches. It's just rainwater running off—it's bone dry in the summer. It comes out below the Russian redoubts, and if we make it through the ravine, we'll be *ahead* of the Russian line and in the clear."

Twisting the rain-greased reins in his hands, Samuel turned to Padraig and Wagner. "What do you think?"

Wagner plucked at his whiskers and stared down into the darkness.

Padraig swung down from his saddle, passed his reins to Begley, and peered downhill. "D-does it get any steeper?" His teeth chattered from the cold.

Samuel translated.

Giray shook his head.

Padraig kicked a loose rock and watched it clatter to a stop ten feet below. "The horses can make it, then. And it's not like we've much choice."

Samuel nodded at Kiely. "Are you up for this?"

The slug had gone clean through Kiely's shoulder, so he'd been lucky. He was pallid, his arm in a makeshift sling, but he was alert. "Yes, Lieutenant, I can make it."

"Just won't be able to shake his elbow for a while, Lieutenant," Price quipped, and all except Giray laughed.

Giray looked blankly at Samuel.

Samuel shrugged. A Muslim didn't need to know about that crude activity.

"Well, that settles it." Samuel unslung his rifle and looped it behind his saddle. "I'll be point man, and Corporal Kerr will follow me. Sergeant Major, you take the rear. We don't want anyone surprising us."

Goldie wouldn't budge when Samuel tugged on her bridle. She rolled her eyes and neighed.

Samuel fondled her muzzle. "Come along, old girl, it's just a narrow road. Look, I'm going first." The bit jingled as he tugged the reins again.

Goldie whickered, nuzzled his palm, and took one step and then another. The freezing water swirled two inches up Samuel's boots as he felt his way forward, scree slithering underfoot and jagged rocks jabbing his leather soles. He continued down the twisting channel, and the biting wind abated, though the rain still funneled down. The gully smelled of salt, wet stone, and moss. The only sounds were the ring of iron shoes on stone, the snap of twigs, and the wheezing of men and horses.

On and on Samuel descended for what seemed like hours—but was logically more like minutes—and soon his calves burned from the strain of the downward inertia and from holding Goldie to a measured step. He caught his boot in a crevice and shifted his weight when pain shot up his leg. His heart raced. A fraction of an inch more, and he'd have twisted or even broken his ankle.

Forty minutes later, he rounded a rocky outcrop to find a lattice of withered branches. "Boughs and debris block the passage," he called back to the others. He repeated his discovery in French.

"Probably washed down by a flash flood." Giray's teeth chattered when he answered.

"Flash flood?" Samuel's fingers tingled. "You said nothing about a flash flood."

"Well, I've never seen one, but I've heard of them," Giray said.

"He's says a flash flood must have washed down the branches." Samuel translated as he tested the nearest branch. His hand closed around it easily—it wasn't too thick—but when he tugged, it wouldn't budge. "Stuck solid. We need to hack them apart with our sabers." He glanced around uneasily, hating to abuse his precious saber, but he saw no other choice.

They backed the horses ten feet up the gully, and leaving Goldie with Padraig, Samuel returned to attack the tangle of branches. He chopped and hacked furiously, praying the rain, the crashing ocean, and the steep walls of the ravine would mask the noise. His wet tunic chaffed his underarms and thighs, and his abraded skin stung worse than the lice bites. So much for the romance of war promised by the burnished parades. He'd give his aching right arm to be sipping wine on the manicured lawns of Springbough Manor.

Soon he was sweltering despite the night chill. He threw off his sable cloak and stepped back to let Padraig take a turn. "Giray, hold my cloak over me so I can strike a lucifer and read my watch." He'd lost track of the time in that dark, rain-sheeted chasm, a narrow channel that had distorted vision, sound, and space.

The wet phosphorus crumbled off the matches as soon as he opened the box. "It's no use, they're all soaked." Damnable rain. Their holster flaps had better keep their powder dry, or the Colts would be useless in a fight. When he noticed he was tugging on his ear, he swore. Childish habit.

Time to make haste; it was imperative they got clear of the
Russian defenses before daybreak. They needed to . . .

". . . through. Lieutenant? Lieutenant, wake up."

He awoke to Padraig shaking him. *Lieutenant?* Why was
Padraig being formal? He was soaked to his bones, shaking, every
muscle aching, and his skin stung all over. Oh God, he was lying
in a gully in Crimea *behind Russian lines.* He sat up and lifted his
face to the rain. Rubbed his eyes. "I must have dozed off."

"Dozed off? You were sleeping as soundly as Bloodyback
Cardigan on his yacht's feather bed."

Even in the near dark Samuel could see that Padraig's face
was ruddy from exposure and effort. The man hadn't taken a
break.

"We're through. Do you want me to lead . . . sir?" Padraig
punctuated the honorific with a pause and a grin.

"No, I'll go first. Well done, Corporal." Samuel returned the
grin. At least it no longer rained.

The canyon took to twisting and turning, but the ground was
more even and still streaming water. When a dog barked—the
deep bay of a big hound—Samuel froze. Had they reached the
end of the canyon? He dropped Goldie's reins and pushed past
her wet flanks to Padraig. "You heard that?"

"What?"

"A dog barking." Samuel drew a circle in the air and added,
"But down here?"

Padraig laughed. "Maybe a seal, but surely not a dog. Have
you been at Giray's booze?"

"Giray's drinking? But he's a Muslim."

"He lives in Russia, so of course he's drinking. But not vodka.
It's some black, rancid—"

The deep woofing returned.

"There, I told you," Samuel said. "Keep the horses quiet. I'll
send Hoffman for a look." He pushed Padraig aside. "Hoffman,
get up here now."

Hoffman had been a poacher before he took the Queen's shilling and could move silently over any ground. He was also handy with the skinning knife he carried in his belt—a fact that several Burmese fighters could have attested to if they were still alive.

Hoffman's eyes were bloodshot, and his stringy hair was plastered across his face. "Sir . . . It's that dog, is it? Very strange. Shall I have a look?"

"Good man. Off you go. Don't go killing an innocent pup, mind you."

"It crossed me mind, sir. A bit o' bow-wow mutton's got to be better than that swill they were feeding us on the boat."

"Get along." A horse pawed the ground, the iron shoe jangling like a bell, startling Samuel. "Control those horses back there," he whispered over his shoulder. "Hush now."

Samuel endured five miserable minutes of scratching, aching, and shaking from the cold before Hoffman materialized at his side like a ragged wraith. "Russian infantry, sir. At the mouth of the canyon."

Damnation. Samuel had hoped to skirt any scouts or Russian patrols.

"I counted six asleep under an outcrop, sir." Hoffman touched the hilt of his knife. "I could have slit their necks, sir, but you told me to come back. Oh yes, sir, the dog. He's there too, sir. A big, black dog, shaggy as—"

"I get the picture. So this is the end of the canyon, then?"

"Appears so, sir. There's a copse of trees, but I couldn't see beyond it."

Samuel regretted his now-blunt saber. Still, there were only six of them and all sleeping. He rolled his shoulders in his customary pre-battle ritual and drew his saber. "Right. Hoffman, *now* you can kill them. And the corporal and I will help."

"Sure I will." Padraig drew his saber from its heavy scabbard. Samuel and Padraig had broken army rules by lining their scabbards with wood to avoid blunting their blades, but now the blades were dull anyway. "But this bloody thing is only good as a club now."

Samuel crept after Hoffman ghosting down the canyon in the rain. Hoffman stopped at the second bend and held up one hand. Samuel's breath came in shallow pants, and he squeezed the worn grip of his saber.

Hoffman darted around the corner, and Samuel followed.

In the grassy clearing, six bundles lay around a pile of charred wood beneath a rock jutting out from the craggy canyon face, a rock shaped like the devil's nose, hook and all. There was no sign of the dog, and Hoffman was already heading for the soldiers on the left. Padraig tiptoed to the men in the middle, and Samuel would take the sleeping men on the right. He and Padraig were expert swordsmen, they had trained from child-hood, and this night—with sleeping victims—would be child's play.

Samuel swung his saber, cut one man's neck to the bone, and hacked down on the second soldier's head. With a *crunch*, blood and brains sprayed the flattened grass. There was no time for regrets in war, and by the time Samuel turned around, they were all dead. Not one had uttered a sound.

Padraig stooped to clean his saber on a Russian's coat. "Damnation, I almost—"

A savage growl cut him off, and Samuel's gaze skittered a few yards to the west.

The largest hound he'd ever seen—bigger than an Irish wolfhound—crouched at the edge of the clearing, its slobbering lips peeled back into a snarl. The hair rose on the nape of Samuel's neck even before the dog charged, but charge it did. Samuel thrust out his saber and braced as the hound loped through the wild grass, covering two yards with each stride.

A whistle trilled out, and the dog stopped.

"Here doggy, over here. Come to Jamie. Here, some meat." Begley sauntered out of the darkness.

The dog wagged its tail and trotted over to Begley.

"Well, I'll be buggered," Padraig said, lowering his bloody saber. "I've never seen the likes of that trickery."

Samuel's legs were suddenly jelly, and it was all he could do not to plop down beside his victims. He waved the hand that still clutched his saber. "You know how he is with horses. Guess he's the same with dogs."

The clouds parted, and moonlight sparkled on the wet grass.

Samuel stooped to examine the dead. "Red cap, brown coat, red trousers, and—"

"Seventeenth Division," Padraig rattled off without hesitation.

Anyone else would have been surprised, but Samuel knew that if not for the discrimination against Irish Catholics, Padraig would have made a name for himself already. Samuel smiled.

He inspected the dead Russians. Why were they there? Giray had said the path would lead them below the Russian positions.

Padraig threw down the musket he was examining. "This shite couldn't hit a town hall at fifty yards. The Russkies are in for a surprise when they see the rifles our boys have now. A thousand paces in the hands of a sharpshooter like my—"

"Hush, I'm trying to think. Why are they down here?" Samuel ran across the clearing and through the thicket of trees, and Padraig followed him.

The gently rolling quilt of meadow and planted fields stretched down to a narrow river flowing west like a moon-silvered thread.

The Alba.

"We *are* below the Russians; there's nobody else down there. Thank God, we made it." Samuel hurried back to the clearing. "Hoffman, bring the others down. Hurry."

Fifteen minutes later, Samuel coaxed Goldie into the Alma River and shuddered when the icy water filled his boots. At the center of the river, the water reached to his ankles. He gasped. "It's fordable, men. The allies can cross anywhere."

"Even the infantry can get through this," Padraig said from

behind Samuel. "Though the Highlanders won't enjoy getting their pretty tartan petticoats wet. Well done, sir. We're in the clear."

Tension drained from Samuel. They'd slipped past the Russian lines, and now it was only a short ride to the British camp. "What good fortune. Only one more river to cross." He'd done it. He'd brought his men back. Every damned one of them.

"The Bulganak," chimed in the know-it-all. "I can't wait to get a hot cup of tea. With the milk poured in last and not first as the daft British make tea."

Samuel edged Goldie closer to Giray's mount. "I remember from the map the Bulganak is in the valley beyond that hill ahead. Can we cross the valley without using the Sevastopol road?"

Grief etched Giray's face, and he was swaying in the saddle from exhaustion or too much drink or both. "Yes, there are meadows, cornfields, and a few orchards on both sides of the road."

"Thank you." Samuel reached out and touched his arm. "It'll get better, I promise you. Time will ease your pain. Come along now. Keep up with me."

They rode north in loose order, with the black hound gamboling around Begley like a puppy. The cords unknotted in Samuel's neck as he focused on the billion stars pricking the vast Russian sky. Colonel Lawrence had cheated him out of his promotion before, but when he delivered vital intelligence—the coast cliffs at Alma were scalable, the infantry could ford the river, and great guns crouched behind two Russian redoubts— Lord Raglan might be the one to promote him.

He led his band up through a vineyard to the crest of another ridge and dismounted. "Corporal, with me. The rest of you stay below the skyline."

The ground was muddy as they climbed, and the tang of rotting grapes tainted the air. Excited to see the lay of the land, Samuel topped the crest and froze. The ground dropped into a narrow valley before rising to another ridge, and thousands of Russian soldiers filled the valley south of the Bulganak River. One full division had advanced to surprise the allies. There was cavalry too, both hussars and Cossacks. Two thousand of them.

And Samuel and his lancers were still trapped.

CHAPTER SIX

September 19, 1854, after midnight

Padraig whistled softly and laid one hand over the other on the pommel of his saddle. "There are few moments in a man's existence when he experiences so much ludicrous distress as when he is in pursuit of his own hat."

"What?" Samuel snapped.

"Dickins. *The Pickwick Papers*. Means we're buggered."

Buggered they were, and the allied army would be in a similar untenable position when morning broke. Samuel's body dragged heavily as the half-moon slid from the clouds and silvered light danced on the myriad bayonets and lances in the valley below.

No, he'd never give up. He'd made a promise to get them back to the regiment, and he'd keep that promise. He pulled out his pocket watch. "Damnation, three in the morning already." The night was almost over, and in the morning the allies would march—bands, bagpipes, and all—into a Russian ambush. Samuel drew a deep breath and exhaled slowly. "We need another way around them." He twisted in the saddle. "Giray. Where's Giray?"

After a moment, Wagner spoke from the rear of the ranks. "He's back here, sir. Half rats he is, sir. Sorry, sir, but I didn't know he had drink on him."

Just as well. Otherwise the sergeant major likely would have joined Giray in his cups. Samuel could kick himself for not confiscating the alcohol, but Giray had needed something to ease his grief. "Send the fool up here." Samuel tapped his saddle while he waited.

Giray rode well enough, but his lopsided smile was a give-away. "Lieutenant, do you need something? I dare—"

"Give me the drink." Samuel held out a blood-spattered hand.

Giray's forehead wrinkled. "I don't have vodka."

"Give it to me. Look, I'm sorry about Taliba, sorry for your troubles, but if you don't pull yourself together, many men will die, *including us*."

Giray cursed in Russian and handed Samuel a wine sack.

Popping the cork, Samuel sniffed the neck of the sack, and the acrid fetor caught in his throat. "Disgusting. What is it?"

"Kvass." Geary hiccupped. "Made from bread."

"Bread!" Padraig piped up. "I can't see bread getting you drunk."

"It's fermented bread." Samuel poured out the thick, foul-smelling liquid and threw the sack on the ground. "We need another way around."

Eyes widening as he viewed the host below, Giray hesitated before saying, "Not through there."

"Obviously."

"The only other way is down the sea cliff and along the coast-line. But we can't take the horses."

Samuel sagged in the saddle. He couldn't leave Goldie behind; he'd had her for years. He couldn't leave her to be abused by a Russian bandit or filthy Cossack. He stared blankly at the Russians in the valley.

Padraig nudged his horse closer. "We've no choice. It's Goldie you're thinking about, isn't it? It's her or us." He cocked a thumb north, toward the Russian army. "We can't face them. If we set her free, she might find you after the battle. Dad says horses are canny that way."

A bit clinked—Price's mount tossing her head. Beside Price, Kiely watched Samuel intently, his face pale in the moonlight. "Very well, let's do it. Lead the way, Giray."

They rode back west, and the rolling meadows soon gave way to low hills veined with gullies and then sandy turf at the coast. Giray turned south and led them between stunted, wind-bent trees in search of a descent that wouldn't kill them. Samuel's heart grew heavier with every step, and he repeatedly ran a hand through Goldie's silver mane. After all they'd been together— hunting in Clonakilty, drilling with Jerry, and fighting on the far side of the world—could he really abandon her in this hostile land? "Don't worry, Goldie, we've still got an hour. I'll think of something." But his assurance rang false in the chill of the night. Soon he'd have to say goodbye.

An hour later Giray reined in at a craggy ledge where seagull droppings glittered like splashes of molten silver on the sand- stone. The sea boomed against the rocks one hundred feet below as they searched the craggy face for a place to climb down. Red and purple crabs scattered before Goldie's hooves, claws clicking on the rocks, and Goldie shied from them.

The icy wind—tasting like salt, smelling like seaweed and fish —ruffled Samuel's cloak as he dismounted. "Right, boys, leave your lances, unsaddle the horses, and don't forget your cartridge boxes."

"Leave me lance," Hoffman griped. "How can I be a lancer without me lance? I'd rather cut off me prick."

"That's because it's useless," Price said. "Good only for shag- ging sheep."

Begley was down on one knee, petting the dog. "And what of Tiny? I can't leave him behind."

The sandy earth twitched beneath Samuel, faint as a tickle,

and he froze. Icy fingers slid down his spine, and he craned around.

A throng of riders—shaggy, shadowed centaurs—cantered toward them from a canyon between the low hills, lances glistening in the moonlight. Several men shouted.

Samuel's heart kicked faster. The Cossacks had caught them.

A loud roar filled the salty air, and the Cossacks broke into a gallop.

"Holy Mary, Mother of God." Padraig stepped back.

Wagner caught Padraig's elbow and pulled him back from the cliff's edge. "Watch it, Kerr. You'll fall over."

Samuel did a lightning assessment of the men. All but one were ready for his command. Kiely trembled, looking terribly young, little more than a schoolboy out of his depth on a strip of sand that would soon turn red from slaughter.

Samuel counted nineteen Cossacks. Three to one, and they likely had fresh horses, whereas the lancers' mounts had endured a rough sea voyage, a rougher landing, and had found no time to rest. He had no chance of outrunning them.

Even as options chased one another across Samuel's thoughts, the Cossacks rumbled closer, a scary quarter mile away, men and horses bobbing with menace. It was obvious who they were hunting, and no doubt the charming Colonel Orlov led them.

Well, Samuel would not make it easy for him, but the cliff top was too open. He called out, "Saddle up, lads. We have to fight. But this isn't the place. We'll lead them between the bluffs where they must bunch up and can't outflank us."

He vaulted onto Goldie, and tired as his girl was, she surged gamely away, south along the cliffs.

"South again," Padraig said from behind him. "I told you we'd be in Sevastopol long before their lordships."

The black dog barked, enjoying the game as it bounded behind Begley. The rhythm of Goldie's grunts sped up, and her muscles rippled between Samuel's thighs as she lengthened her strides. Equipment clinked and jingled as the lancers followed close behind. Samuel touched the reins, and Goldie turned between two sandy bluffs, into a narrow valley only thirty feet wide.

Samuel ran Goldie another hundred yards before he raised his hand. "Halt!"

The lancers reined in, and their lathered mounts pranced to a standstill.

"Kiely, pass me your lance. Stay here with Giray; you can use your Colt." Samuel edged Goldie over to Kiely and grabbed his lance. The thick ash was hard and reassuring in his hand.

"When they reach the corner, couch lances and charge before they've time to organize. As soon as you strike, drop your lance and shoot for all you're worth."

All breathless, they looked at him with wild eyes, and for once nobody had a flippant comment.

"You're lancers, men, the best there is. Professionals worth any three of those irregulars. I don't know about you, but I'd rather die here, fighting for the hope of escape, than freeze to death in a Siberian prison."

Padraig hooted and punched the air. "Right you are. Death or glory."

"Death or glory," all bellowed together.

Wagner wheeled about and rode to the left flank. "For the regiment, for the Queen."

"Piss on the Queen," Padraig said in Spanish as he closed up with Samuel. "For the regiment and for us."

Goldie threw up her head and sidestepped, feeding off the excitement.

The tic started under his left eye as Samuel rolled his shoulders. He blinked it off. "Kiely, Giray, wait here, and if we fall on the charge, ride on through the canyon. Thank you and good luck to you."

"Bloody madness, isn't it," Padraig said in Spanish. "We've no hope."

"There's always hope. Kill as many as you can, and I'll hope I kill even more." Samuel undid the flap of his holster, slid his saber out six inches, and dropped it back. He passed his lance to Padraig. "Hold this a minute."

The chink of harnesses and the thump of hooves sounded in the distance, and Goldie tugged for her head. He checked her with the reins, patted her neck—as much to reassure himself as her—unslung his carbine, and aimed for the end of the bluff. "Steady, lads, and keep close. Stirrup to stirrup."

The horde of Cossacks swept around the bluff like a gray wave, and Samuel fired. A horse stumbled and fell, throwing its rider. The man screamed as a following horse tripped over him, knocking another horse aside, and both of their riders hurtled from their saddles, dark lances flying.

He slung his carbine over his shoulder, snatched the lance from Padraig, and couched it. "Charge! *Death or glory!*"

He leaned forward as Goldie surged ahead, her silver mane billowing in the moonlight, her breath whooshing rhythmically. The red and white pennant fluttered as he steadied the wavering lance on a squat Cossack in the center of the pack. Clumps of wet sand flicked from Goldie's hooves, and Samuel rose and fell with her gallop, the familiar rhythm focusing him.

It was the last thing the Cossacks might have expected, a handful of men charging them without hesitation, and they had no time to prepare before Samuel punched his lance through the squat Cossack's chest. Despite his knees clamping Goldie with all his strength, the shock almost unseated him. He swayed back, righted himself, and drew his Colt, the Cossack's scream blaring in his ear.

He shot another rider out of the saddle, cocked, and shot again. Men screamed, and the Colts thundered, firing over and over. Thank God for those six-shot revolvers. His last shot pierced the face of a hollow-cheeked man and blew a mist of blood into the air. The Cossack's horse spun away as the man fell from the saddle.

Samuel tossed the Colt to his left and drew his saber as he broke through the Cossack line, where riderless horses plunged past him. He wheeled Goldie, and she charged the Cossacks from behind. He rose in the stirrups and slashed at a rider's arm. Blunt or not, his blade cut the man to the bone. The Cossack let out a piercing scream as he tumbled, so close that Samuel smelled his fetid breath.

Moonlight glittered on their sweeping sabers as the lancers whirled among the remaining mounted Cossacks. Goldie shouldered aside a horse, and Samuel slashed open its rider's side. As Goldie bit the neck of another horse, a lancer's blade exploded out of her rider's stomach. When the Cossack was punched from his saddle, Samuel glimpsed Price's snarling face behind him.

A Colt barked in the distance. *Kiely.* Samuel whirled.

Two Cossacks charging Kiely threw out their arms like marionettes and tumbled from their horses, and Kiely swung his smoking revolver to cover the melee. The valley stank of sweat, shit, and blood. Screams and the ring of sabers filled the air.

Goldie shuddered when a burly Cossack charged his horse into her, almost unseating Samuel. He clamped on with his knees as the big Cossack swung his sword and threw up his blade to ward off the attack. The shock of the blow shot up his arm, but he was in the flow of battle; his world slowed, giving him the time he needed.

The Cossack was a monster, with pendulous jowls, a tangled beard, and long legs that almost brushed the ground.

Samuel was faster and far more skillful. A touch from his toe and heel, and Goldie danced around the Cossack, allowing Samuel to stab him in the gut. The blade slid deep. He twisted it and then ripped up. The Cossack shrieked and crumpled from his saddle, banging into the earth. His horse raced off, dragging him up the gully, his head slamming against the ground.

Goldie snapped at a horse on her left, and it shied away with a whinny. In a thrice Samuel urged her forward, rose in the stirrups, and hacked at the rider's neck. Warm blood sprayed his face, tasting metallic on his tongue, and splashed Goldie's neck.

A blow to his side winded Samuel—a Cossack sword—and he swung his saber across Goldie's head to slash the face of the Cossack who'd struck him. A saber flashed from nowhere and carved down through the man's head, sheepskin hat and all.

Padraig yanked the Cossack from the saddle, and the body crashed to the ground. "That's the last of them."

The guns were silent, but the screams of wounded men and horses filled the gully and Begley's dog barked nonstop. The tangled pile of Cossacks writhed and groaned at Samuel's feet, and he retched. Padraig was still in the saddle but pale, his right arm bloody from hand to elbow and his mouth hanging open. Begley, Price, and the sergeant major were bloody too but appeared unharmed.

"My God." Kiely was still behind him, and Samuel wheeled around. Kiely's face was black with powder, and he was reloading his Colt with shaking hands.

"Where's Hoffman?" Samuel spurred Goldie around the fallen men. Dear God, let him be alive.

"Here. Over here." Padraig was already kneeling by Hoffman. "He took a lance in his leg, and he's pouring blood. Begley, quick, man."

Samuel cantered to Hoffman and dismounted as Begley arrived. Hoffman's pantaloons were torn and bloodied at the thigh where a lance had sliced through his leg, and Samuel's flesh crawled. That white stuff beneath the torn flesh was bone.

Begley cut away the cloth, and Hoffman groaned as he prodded around the wound. "It missed the arteries, but it's chipped the bone." Begley produced one of the bandages he carried and began gently wrapping the leg. "Don't worry, mate, you'll live."

"Hear that, Hoffman? You're going to be fine." Samuel patted Hoffman's chest and rose. Pain stabbed his side, reminding him of the blow he took, and he reached down. The cloak was intact.

He slipped his hand inside and gingerly felt his side. He was damp with sweat, but there was no blood. The blow had bruised him, but the Cossack blade had failed to pierce the heavy cloak.

"Rabbits will be happy to hear the poacher's out of the game for a while." Padraig stood and caught Samuel's elbow. "Was it Orlov? He seems hell-bent on capturing us."

"I don't know." Samuel looked for the other lancers. They were dragging wounded Cossacks clear of the dead. "Anyone see that officer from yesterday, the one with the cheroot?"

"Aghh, the bastard's not here." Price was holding a bloody cloth to a wounded Cossack's breast. Samuel would never have marked the Liverpudlian as a compassionate man.

If the Russian colonel wasn't there, was he with another band hunting them? If so, why were the Cossacks so eager to catch a handful of lost lancers? Something didn't add up. Regardless, Samuel was taking his men down that cliff. He stooped and wiped his saber on a fallen Cossack's coat. The quick swipe wouldn't take all the blood off, but hopefully it would be clean enough not to stick in the scabbard.

He returned to Begley and Hoffman. "How is he?"

Begley's forehead wrinkled. "He'll be fine if we get him to a doctor before the wound festers, but he can't walk, that's for sure." He frowned up at Samuel. "There's no way he can climb down that cliff."

If Hoffman couldn't descend the cliff, they were trapped again. Damn their luck.

"Then we're buggered." Wagner rubbed his face with bloody hands.

Begley looked at Samuel, eyes bloodshot and skin pale. "Leave me here, sir. B-b-better just one of us ends up in a Russian prison than . . . than all of us."

"Not a chance of that," Padraig snapped.

Samuel rolled his neck and stared blankly into the distance. He didn't have many choices, and not a single good one. "Round up the Cossack horses; we'll take them with us. We need extra mounts, and without horses, the survivors can't raise the alarm."

"All of them?" Padraig scanned the canyon. "Their horses have scattered. Some could be halfway to Sevastopol al—"

"As many as you can. Just leave none here."

Samuel unslung his carbine to reload it. His men would don Cossack coats, and he would lead them directly through the Russian lines. And if they were stopped, they'd fight their way through. Better that than to die in a Russian prison.

CHAPTER SEVEN

September 19, 1854, before dawn

Why are those flunkies more important than me? Orlov paced outside
the enormous green tent in the darkness and fired another
glance at the heavy flaps. General Kiriakoff was doing this delib-
erately to teach him who was in charge. He brushed his hand
down his sodden frock coat, and shame heated his face. That
bastard serf had scorched it for naught. He checked the watch in
his hand again. Five o'clock. Damn it, why had Kiriakoff's
minions roused him so early if the wretch wouldn't meet him?

Reeking of char, unwashed flesh, and horse dung, the hasty
camp bustled as infantry filled in their abandoned sleeping holes;
serf soldiers didn't deserve the luxury of tents. Those who had
finished their labors hunched around feeble campfires, stirring
bowls of soup made from rotten cabbage and garlic, many
coughing and hacking up phlegm. Gallopers tended skinny
horses or warmed themselves by fizzling fires as the sound of
drunken singing drifted down the hillside.

His eyes tightened. Rabble. It was a wonder they hadn't
dragged along their disgusting sprawl of camp followers—

whores, camp wives, and ill-begotten spawn. They hadn't had time, that was why. The scum would catch up soon enough.

At long last a redheaded lieutenant in a mud-splattered white uniform marched from the tent in his fancy boots and clicked his heels in front of Orlov. It had stopped raining some time ago, but it was biting cold. The lieutenant looked like one of those soft city aristocrats, pale and fresh-faced, not hard like that flinty-eyed lancer Orlov had escaped earlier. Now, that Britisher had been a bastard. His men too; they'd fought like wildcats. Good Cossacks were dead because of that devil. Some of his best men.

The lieutenant stiffened, his head and shoulders thrown back, his elbows almost touching his spine, and saluted. "Colonel Orlov, General Kiriakoff will see you now."

The lieutenant was short and round with a receding hairline, a pocked face, and stupid blue eyes. Just one more fool placed in a position of authority for no reason other than who his father was. Orlov looked up at the rain-filled sky and shook his head in what he hoped was a disparaging way.

"Lead on, Lieutenant."

Why hadn't he heard any news from Captain Denisov? With a hundred riders searching the grasslands, they should have killed the lancers by now. He tightened the hand behind his back into a fist. If Maxwell was right and they'd seen him signaling . . . Prince Menshikov would blame him if his cousin was discovered spying, and Menshikov was not a forgiving man.

A soft puff of heat met him when the lieutenant opened the tent flap. Inside, a handful of senior officers lounged around the fire blazing in a burnished brazier, quaffing vodka or brandy and smoking cigarettes. A fellow with silver hair sat at a table, pouring over a map weighted down with two swords. General Kiriakoff—who else could he be—was about sixty and lean, with a long shriveled face. He sat erect in a fancy blue uniform dripping gold braid and medals—it was easy to fool people with fine cloth and tin.

The murmured conversations ceased, and aloof eyes fixed on the barbarian count from the hard eastern lands of Azov. Orlov stepped into a wide stance with his arms loose at his sides, breathing the haze of smoke and body odor. Had any of these indolent officers heard of a sauna or even a bath?

"Colonel Orlov, I hope your intelligence is good. Moving my accommodation and staff on short notice was disruptive." Kiriakoff waved a hand over notes on the corner of the table—the notes Orlov had passed from Maxwell? "Major Dyomin over there had hoped to win back his wager in a hand of whist tonight. Instead we're stuck out here between Lord Raglan's army and the prince's artillery."

Someone should have told the old goat he was campaigning and that he should have left his circus tent back in Sevastopol.

"I'm sorry for your inconvenience, General." Like hell he was. If only his hideous tent would blow over. "But this is an opportunity to wipe Raglan's cavalry off the board." Perhaps that fawning Dyomin would have liked to take a wager on that outcome. Or even Kiriakoff himself. Kiriakoff didn't seem to have much confidence in Orlov's plan to ambush the enemy cavalry. "Our source informed us that the Heavy Brigade has yet to land their horses in Calamita Bay, and the Light Brigade is the only cavalry the allies have. If we can eliminate them tomorrow, Raglan will be blind."

"*If.* A big if until we get reinforcements of our own." Kiriakoff glanced at his staff for support. "Raglan's army outnumbers our forces. We were safe south of the Alma, sheltering behind our artillery."

"We have two thousand Cossack riders down here, sir, and the infantry is well entrenched, supported by horse artillery." Moscow peacock; Kiriakoff hadn't a clue. "The Cossacks will lure the British cavalry into the trap. When we wipe them out, we can fall back behind the Alma. With the British cavalry eliminated, our cavalry will play havoc on the allies' left flank."

"I didn't appreciate your going behind my back to General

Menshikov. Once again you've lived up to your reputation as a troublesome man."

"I've campaigned with Prince Menshikov before, but I don't know you." This truth might infuriate Kiriakoff, but Orlov didn't have time to dance around. The trap would be sprung today or never. There was no way he'd let Kiriakoff steal his chance for glory.

Kiriakoff's tiny nostrils flared. "I don't know you, *sir*. You may be a count, but I'm a general, and you'll respect that. Perhaps you spend too much time with your . . . Cossacks. I should recommend a reassignment to a more professional regiment, like the Kievsky Hussars. You might learn some discipline there."

Orlov's muscles quivered. The regular army put more emphasis on drilling and the appearance of the troops than on battle worthiness. Oh, they could posture and march, but the men couldn't even fire a musket. That lot was nothing but cannon fodder.

"General, the Cossack cavalry has been the tip of Russia's spear for decades. I'll—"

"Enough, Colonel." Kiriakoff's fingers curled on the table, and someone sniggered behind Orlov. "Your contempt for our regular forces is well known and not appreciated. Now, you distracted me. Ah, yes, I remember. Your men are roaming all over the steppes tonight. Why is that?"

"I'm not at liberty to say, sir. It's a mission for General Menshikov himself."

Kiriakoff's nostrils flared again. "Well, the enemy column scattered from here back to Calamita Bay, but we expect them in the afternoon. Your men better be back before then. That's all." He turned back to his map.

"Thank you . . . General." Orlov snapped a lazy salute, wheeled, and strode from the tent, ignoring the smirking faces in the fire's light. Afternoon. That gave him time to ride out and discover why Denisov hadn't dealt with the British lancers.

Lieutenant Galdin waited outside Orlov's tent, wringing his hands. "Colonel, bad news, I'm afraid." Galdin cringed like a dog fearing a blow.

Orlov ran a hand through his hair. "What is it now, man?"

Galdin, jumpy, peered around and then sidled closer to Orlov. "Someone's waiting by your campfire, sir. It might be more private there."

"Pah. Let's go." This had something to do with the cursed British, his bones were telling him.

He didn't know the name of the bloodied Cossack being bandaged by another Cossack, but the face was familiar. One of Denisov's men, perhaps.

The Cossack's lip trembled when the man saw Orlov. "Sir, the British lancers attacked us. We fought hard and courageously, but there were too many of them." He looked away. "At least twenty."

The bastard took him for a fool. Orlov's pulse sped up, and he lashed the Cossack across the face with his nagaika. A bloody welt blossomed on the Cossack's cheek as he fell to his knees with a scream.

"Liar. There were only a handful, six or seven at the most. Denisov is your commander, no?"

The Cossack lay beside the fire where a kettle boiled furiously on a tripod. He clutched his cheek, eyes wild, and said nothing.

"Galdin, pick the wretch up. Where's your commander?"

The Cossack's fresh bandage was soaked with blood, and blood poured from the gash on his cheek. "D-dead, sir. Captain Denisov is dead. Most of them are dead. I left five wounded men back on the coast, and I could find only one horse. The British are devils, sir, and their guns . . . They never run out of bullets. They just keep firing and firing."

"Of course they run out of bullets, idiot. They're six-shooters. Where exactly did this happen?"

"Five, s-six miles from here, by the cliffs. They're in the second or third canyon."

"Galdin, inform Major Yelagin that I want Troop D ready to ride in ten minutes. Have someone take this wretch to the sawbones."

Orlov ground his teeth and stalked to his haversack to retrieve his spare pistol. He had to catch or kill the lancers before General Menshikov learned they still roamed free *and* he had to get back before noon to bait the trap for the Light Brigade.

He checked his pocket watch by the light of the watch fire. Already five thirty. A curse on Denisov for his failure. "Aghh, to hell with this clown's army." He kicked the kettle off the tripod and listened as it rattled down the hill.

CHAPTER EIGHT

September 19, 1854, before dawn

An hour after the battle on the cliffs, Samuel patted his Cossack horse, trying to build rapport with the animal, as they rode down through vineyards and orchards east of the coastal road from Eupatoria to Sevastopol. Goldie trailed behind him. It was bad luck they couldn't have climbed down the cliffs, but this way he got to keep Goldie. To the west, one redoubt sat on Telegraph Hill, an unfinished semaphore hanging above it like a gibbet, and east of the road the second redoubt, also bristling with artillery, sat on the flat-topped summit known as Kourgane Hill. He wrung the greasy reins and peered ahead. They were advancing without a scout again. But only Giray spoke Russian, and Samuel needed him close. If one of the others scouted ahead and encountered a checkpoint, he wouldn't be able to speak. They were safer staying together.

Hoffman rode up from behind. "Sir, I'm afraid I'm slowing you down. Leave me. I don't want you caught because of me."

"Nobody gets left behind. Don't bring it up again."

Hoffman nodded and fell back to the other lancers.

Samuel gestured to Padraig. "This will work. We're dressed as Cossacks, and Giray will do the talking if we're stopped."

"It better work." Padraig whipped off the sheepskin hat and scratched his head vigorously. "If they kill me and bury me in this awful outfit, I'll haunt you in the next life. Know what? I'm going to throw this flea-riddled hat away."

"No." Seeing Padraig's action, Giray spoke for the first time since they had left the cliffs. "The sheepskin hats make us look like Kuban Cossacks from Ural. If they take us for strangers, our unfamiliarity with the area is explained."

"Keep the hat on," Samuel translated.

"What about the sentries on the bridge?" Padraig asked. "Are you sure we shouldn't ford the river further down?"

"It would appear too suspicious. We must be bold and cross the bridge as scouts would," Samuel answered.

Wagner plucked at his sideburns as he squinted. "Agreed, but we should take only our own horses and leave the others here."

Samuel headed for a thicket of trees. "All right, lads, change to your own horses over there." It was unlikely they'd be spotted in the small hours of the morning with all eyes facing northward toward the allied army, and their horses had enjoyed at least a brief respite.

"Come along, Tiny." Begley whistled to the black mastiff rooting beneath a grapevine.

A thousand smoldering campfires and watch fires scattered across the orchards and vineyards were stern reminders that they rode through the heart of enemy territory, and Samuel rubbed his hands down his trousers as he eyed the path ahead. He was out of his mind if he thought riding down the coastal road, right through enemy defenses, would work, but he'd no choice.

The village of Burliuk was a collection of battered wooden houses and a few finer houses that Giray said were the summer residences of wealthy folk from Sevastopol, all clustered around a white church with gold-painted domes. They rode through without slowing.

"Typical that the church has all the money," Padraig said. "Must be Protestants."

"Shush. Only Giray talks from now on." Samuel tapped his fingers on the reins. Padraig was a gem, but sometimes he'd no notion of danger.

Several of the houses were boarded up, and the village was dark. The occupants wouldn't be happy with the brush and chopped wood stacked along their walls, ready to be set alight if the British made it to the river.

The horses' hooves drummed on the timber bridge on the far side of the village as they rode across, and the narrow river whispered below. Ahead of them, five soldiers in greatcoats and red forage caps warmed themselves by the watch fires burning on either side of the road.

A lean sergeant with a black mustache stepped from one fire, straddled the road, and rumbled something in Russian. Giray straightened in the saddle and barked back at him. The sergeant frowned, crossed his arms, and studied them before narrowing his eyes at the village behind them. When he spoke again, his voice grated like a whetstone across a blade. Something Giray had said must have angered him; they were going to have to shoot their way through. Samuel slid his hand closer to his holster. He'd undone the flap earlier, just in case.

Giray slapped the Cossack whip against the palm of his hand and cut the sergeant off with a loud retort. Samuel's weary head throbbed again. Why was Giray provoking the sergeant? If only Samuel could understand.

The sergeant turned his head the merest fraction, and the men by the watch fires tensed as one soldier scurried over. The sergeant rattled something harsh, and the soldier ran past Samuel onto the bridge, heading for the village.

Samuel clenched his jaw. What had they said? Surely they were rumbled. He closed his hand on the Colt.

The dog must have got bored, for it ran past Samuel and up to the sergeant. The sergeant chuckled, ruffled the dog's enormous black head, and called out to the departing soldier. Samuel cursed under his breath. Damned primitive language; what was happening? The sergeant's features had softened, and his posture had relaxed.

The sergeant spoke to Giray, who bobbed his head and smiled before responding. Samuel turned his ear toward them as if that would help him understand as the sergeant waxed on happily.

Finally Giray said a few cheerful words, saluted the sergeant, and rode on. Samuel sagged in the saddle and nudged Goldie after Giray. His blood pulsed in his ears as the horses plodded down the muddy road. He couldn't wait to hear what Giray had said. He twisted in the saddle. The others were following, and the hound was back trotting beside Begley.

Twenty yards up the road, Giray let out a long breath. "That was close."

Samuel's hands were shaking. "You're telling me. What happened?"

"He asked why we were riding out so early. I scolded him for challenging an officer and ordered him to mind his own business. That didn't sit well with him, and he sent that soldier to fetch the officer of the watch." Giray laughed shakily. "In truth, I thought they'd catch us, but that big dog appeared, and the sergeant knew him. He said he's run away from General Kiriakoff, commander of the sergeant's forward division, and the general has men searching for him. I seized on that and claimed that was exactly what we'd been about and were now returning the dog to Kiriakoff. The sergeant said we were lucky bastards, and Kiriakoff would reward—"

"For heaven's sake." Padraig spoke over him. "What happened back there? Are we clear?"

"Yes, thank God." Samuel smiled slowly and related what had happened to the others. Then he closed up with Giray. "Did he say anything else?"

"I asked him where the general's bivouac was, and he told me much more than that. The general is camped with his men ahead in the next valley—a full infantry division, horse artillery, and two thousand hussars and Cossacks. They expect the allied army in the afternoon and plan to use Cossacks to lure your cavalry into a trap."

Samuel's mouth dropped open. "That must be the Light Brigade. It's not much over thirty-six hours since Maxwell cut us adrift. There's no way the Heavy Brigade has landed yet."

Padraig blew out a forced breath. "What now? What did he say?"

The troopers tittered behind them. Even for the men of C Company who'd witnessed the rare friendship between an officer and an enlisted man, a trooper snapping at his officer was a rare sight.

"Sorry, chaps." Samuel relayed what Giray had said.

"It must be the Light Brigade," Padraig said, "The French have only a few chasseurs in the field yet. Handy fighters, but there can't be more than a hundred of them."

Now they had no choice but to break through; the lives of their comrades depended on it. Samuel's throat tightened as, unconsciously, he nudged Goldie into a trot, and the others matched his pace. The coast road was rutted and muddy, bordered on both sides by vineyards and orchards. An owl hooted twice from an apple tree bowing over the low ditch along the road.

"The allies won't reach the Russian lines until the afternoon." Giray added as an afterthought.

Samuel slowed Goldie again. Haste might draw undue attention. "Then we've time enough. We'll brazen our way thorough before dawn and ride hard until we find the Light Brigade."

Padraig frowned as they rounded a bend in the road. "And what if—"

A twelve-pounder lay askew in the ditch, with a half dozen soldiers loitering at the roadside, watching six others lever up the side without a wheel. One of the cannon's two-horse team lay dead beside it. Samuel's nerves jangled. Of all the cursed luck, and just when they were almost back with their troops. The lads had better not panic.

A clean-shaven officer in a greatcoat raised his hand and barked an order.

Giray muttered, "That captain's demanding we hand over a horse."

The officer stalked up to Samuel and shouted directly at him. Samuel's fingers tightened on the reins. He couldn't reply. He'd play mute and look away. Let Giray respond.

Giray's reply was high-pitched, his voice breaking; his nerve had gone. The officer shouted again, and his men eddied closer to the riders.

Before Samuel could react, the officer dragged him from Goldie and clubbed him. Pain stabbed through his head, bright stars flashed, and he fell into a black tunnel.

———

Hundreds of watch and bivouac fires twinkled on Telegraph Hill and Kourgane Hills in the blue light of dawn, and the northerly breeze rustled the leaves of apple trees bordering the road. The air was fresher, washed clean of smoke, and perfumed with the hint of apples. The rhythmic pulse of his black stallion's chest between Orlov's knees eased his angst. He was going to catch that murdering lieutenant and his lancers, and, after all the Cossacks they'd slaughtered, he was taking no prisoners.

In the distance, shadows scurried back and forth in the road beside a lopsided cannon. He squinted. The scene didn't look right. His pulse quickened as he drew closer, and he heard high-pitched shouts above hoofbeats, the creak of leather, and the jangle of equipment. The stench of blood and death fouled the air, and Major Yelagin's horse stepped sideways beside him.

"Steady, Major. What's going on up there?"

Yelagin yanked his bridle savagely. "Sorry, sir. Her first time. It smells like a slaughterhouse."

Infantrymen were laying out bodies. No, body *parts*. The bodies had been hacked apart.

"Whoa!" Orlov reined in beside a pallid captain, and his Cossacks splashed to a halt in puddles of rainwater behind him. "What happened here?"

The young captain was one of those city types he despised, with his lips all aquiver and his eyes bulging. "They butchered them, sir. Cut them to pieces." The captain shuddered and never once turned toward the carnage.

Orlov didn't have time for this. "Who did this, soldier? Who attacked those gunners? Pull yourself together; you're a Russian officer. Do you want your men to see you sniveling like a whipped trollop? Are there survivors?"

"One. There was one. But he died before w—"

"Did he say who did this?"

"He must have been delirious. He said it was British lancers and—"

"Don't be a fool—British lancers couldn't do this." There'd been only a handful of lancers, not enough to commit this carnage, and no British officer would condone such brutality.

"Tartar rebels too, sir. He said they helped the British."

Tartars had risen all over district. That made more sense, but how had that British officer allowed this? "Did the wounded soldier see which way they went?"

The captain's eyes were bloodshot as he shook his head. "He was too far gone."

Orlov turned to Major Yelagin, who was ogling the row of severed limbs and torsos with bulging eyes. "Check for tracks. I want to know which way the bastards went."

"Yes, sir."

Six riders, the best of Yelagin's scouts, swung down from their skittish ponies and searched the road. Orlov drummed his fingers on his saddle as they worked their way up and down the road and into the orchard on both sides.

He shook his head and muttered, "What the devil is taking so long?" Were the wretches blind?

Five minutes later he could bear it no longer. "Yelagin! Recall them. I want to know what they found."

Yelagin's sharp yell brought the trackers trotting back.

"We figure there were at least twenty, Colonel." Yelagin plucked at his collar. "They split up to ride in all directions, up—"

"They don't want us to find those blasted lancers." Orlov cracked his knuckles. "We'll split up, just as they did. Twenty men in each direction. I doubt they'll risk riding far. Most likely they'll hide in Bulganak and pray that the allies win through to save their cowardly hides. I'll take that direction." He wheeled his horse and raked her flanks. He wouldn't just kill those lancers. They had made a fool of him, and now this—hacking Russians to pieces. He was going to impale them and watch them die slowly.

———

"Samuel, wake up." Cold hands shook him roughly. "For God's sake, wake up."

The ache in his head increased with every shake. His heavy eyelids refused to open. Where was he? He opened his mouth to speak but only moaned. His body shivered.

"Samuel, you all right?" The hands shook him again.

"Leave off." He pushed the hands away.

Who said that? He screamed, the sound vibrating in his chest, and he clamped his hands over his face. They were clammy, stinking of . . .

Blood!

He cringed away, and the bed, mattress—whatever— scratched his sweating back.

"Samuel, you're scaring me." The voice was high-pitched now.

Who was Samuel? He wasn't Samuel. He was . . . His heart jolted. He was . . .

Rough hands pulled his own hands away from his face, gently but firmly. "Can you open your eyes?" The voice shook, sounding distant and disoriented. But it was he who was disoriented.

What had he been doing? He was in a strange place. A foreign place. So what was a familiar place? The air stank of smoke and sweat.

"Maybe the bang on his head made him deaf?" A second voice, accented, had joined the first.

Who were they? Who was *he*? Oh God, his head. He clasped both hands to his skull and squeezed.

Muttering. Someone was muttering. He couldn't understand the words at all.

"Samuel, please open your eyes. We've got to get out of here. It's after seven already; we must keep going."

Was that the first fellow speaking again? He forced his eyes open.

A broad-faced man with rumpled blond hair stared at him with pea-green eyes, his ruddy face tight with concern. "He's awake, lads. Samuel?"

"Who . . . who are you?" His voice was croaky, his mouth parched. "Water?" It seemed a better choice than blurting *who am I?* He was pretty sure he was supposed to know his name.

After he drank, however—and with the eyes of half a dozen unfamiliar men staring at him—he managed, "What's my name?"

The closest stranger ran a big hand through his dirty hair and laughed shakily. "Stop fooling around. We're in a spot of danger here."

He grasped the stranger by both arms. "Am I Samuel? Who are you?"

The ruddy face paled. He could smell the stranger's sweat and the stench of burning wood.

"He's lost his mind."

Another voice murmured in a strange language. He clung to the blond man. "Lost my mind? How?"

An older face pushed close, a round face with brown whiskers and a bald chin. "I saw this back in Prussia. A knock on the head, and the fellow didn't know his name. He never knew it again."

The foreign murmuring droned on behind the two strangers. What had they said about a knock on the head? His stomach churned, and without even moving, he grew dizzy.

"Begley says he's seen it before when a horse kicked a man in the head. His memory came back eventually." The blond man patted the hand clinging to his sweaty shirt. "It's going to be fine, Samuel. Rest a while. We're leaving soon."

The fellow stepped back. "Begley, stay with him. Price, saddle the horses."

The voices droned and barked until the words themselves had no meaning.

"Wait you here—Ivan come back soon. We take you to the road."

His eyes were like lead. He couldn't keep them open. His head ached.

He escaped into darkness.

CHAPTER NINE

September 19, 1854, early morning

He woke to a jumbled monologue, foreign words he didn't understand spoken by a single voice. His head pounded, and his body itched all over. He jammed his hands under his armpits, hugged himself tightly, and forced his gummy eyes open. A smoke-blackened, thatched ceiling sat on a low stone wall. How'd he get to that strange place? He shut his eyes, and the vignette of a lofty molded ceiling and bay windows overlooking a tranquil green sea flashed before him. *That* was familiar. *That* was where he belonged. He reached for his aching head and felt a bandage. He'd injured himself. He shifted. His entire body ached.

The unintelligible susurration droned continuously. Curious, he rolled his head to look. A wizened man, spare as any scarecrow, was lifting his head skyward and then touching his forehead to the small mat upon which he knelt. He wore strange clothing—a loose garment, something like a nightshirt—and he'd wrapped his feet and legs, toe to knee, with ragged bandages.

Maybe he was dreaming. He blinked rapidly and looked

again. The old man was still there, murmuring on in that small room where a crude table leaned lopsided against the wall and three stools stood beside a feeble fire.

"You're awake, sir. Hoffman, he's awake."

He started. He hadn't seen the two soldiers seated by the window. They were dressed in blue uniforms—a pale youth with blue eyes, one arm in a sling, and a man with stringy hair, a bloody bandage wrapped around his leg. He knew the uniform, and the men, too, were familiar, their names floating in the back of his jumbled mind, just out of reach.

The youth sat forward, observing him keenly. "Are you feeling better, sir? That Russian officer gave you an awful knock on the head."

Russian officer . . . Why would he do that? Enemies. The Russians were enemies.

Rough straw scratched his back, and he shifted on his cot. The smoky room smelled of rotting cabbage and garlic, making him both queasy and hungry. "I know you. So that means you know me."

"Trooper Kiely, sir. Seventeenth Lancers. And you're Lieutenant Samuel Kingston. That blow to your head must have scrambled your brain."

Yes, he was Samuel. Samuel Kingston. Thank God. "Russian officer? Where are we?"

"A village called Bulganak, in the home of one of the Tartars who rescued us from those Russian gunners. Bloody savages, those Tartars are. Charged in, slaughtered every one of the Russians, and hacked them to pieces. I don't mind telling you, sir, I retched until I almost fainted."

He wasn't going insane. Samuel slumped back as he remembered he was in Crimea. At war.

The other soldier stirred and rubbed the scar over his eye. "Hoffman, sir. Do you remember me?"

Samuel searched the abyss of his mind for the still-elusive names. "Almost. Vaguely."

"When that officer slugged you, sir," Hoffman continued, "we began shooting, but they outnumbered us and would have captured us. A dozen Tartar rebels charged in, pistols blazing, swords flashing, and killed them all. When it was over, the one who spoke English told us the Russians deserved that treatment for murdering their families."

"He said the Russians are exterminating their people, sir," the younger soldier added. "Literally killing entire families and clans. They hate the Russkies something terrible."

"Why are we here? Do you—"

The door swung open, and an overweight man with thin strands of black hair pasted over his bald head hurried inside, sweating in his twill frock. Two soldiers followed, a tall staff officer behind them, but it was the last man in—a muscular, blond corporal—who jogged free his memory.

He saw—felt—the wind stirring the reflection of beech trees, yellow gorse, and purple bracken on a tidal lake. He heard a pistol shot. A blond boy, fifteen years old, held the smoking pistol with which he'd saved Samuel's life. A cowardly aristocrat, a man in his twenties, clutched his wounded shoulder beside the quay.

"Padraig!"

Padraig's eyes lit up. "Your memory's back. Thank the Blessed Virgin."

Samuel had a fleeting thought that they'd both pay for that ancient duel someday, and then the officer spoke.

"I say, how dare you speak to an officer like that, Corporal. I'll hear you address him as sir, or I'll have you flogged."

The colonel's clipped voice reminded Samuel of the boys in boarding school, full of arrogance. He was about thirty and as tall as Padraig. His greasy, yellow hair was swept back from his prominent brow, and red-blond sideburns covered his ruddy jowls.

Samuel definitely didn't know *him*.

Padraig flushed. "Sorry, sir, a slip of the tongue, that's all. I got excited to see the Lieutenant's remembering himself.

"He means no insolence, Colonel." Samuel nodded as the jumbled memories pieced together. They'd been sneaking through the Russian lines. "Apparently I was injured in a skirmish, but I remember nothing of the incident. May I ask how you, a staff officer, find yourself here?"

The colonel took a step back and licked his lips. "I'm Colonel Albert Lillingston of the Coldstream Guards and attached to Lord Raglan's staff. The widening gap between the British Second Division and the French Third Division concerned Lord Raglan, and he sent me to Prince Napoleon with a request to close the gap. It's rough and unfamiliar country out there, and I must have got turned around. Spotting a troop of cavalry, I rode over for help only to discover they were Kievsky Hussars, and they promptly took me prisoner." He threw his hands up. "I'm shortsighted. Anybody could have made the same mistake."

"And how did you find us, sir?"

"Your men rescued me." The colonel spoke matter-of-factly, seeming to lack appreciation, and pointed at Wagner. "How did you find me, Sergeant Major?"

"Frarat saw them lead you through the village, Colonel." Wagner's accent was thicker than usual, as if addressing a senior officer intimidated him. "And Corporal Kerr insisted we follow you and ambush them outside town. Our Tartar friends helped, always eager for a crack at de Russians, ja."

Wagner smiled at the overweight Tartar wiping blood from his sword and chattering to the old man rolling up his little red mat. "Frarat led the men who appeared from nowhere when we clashed with those Russian gunners. He's always spoiling for a fight."

Frarat. A new ally. Frarat's bushy beard parted to show a small smiling mouth, and the man waddled over to Samuel. "I'm happy meet brave lieutenant who's killing Russians all over hills. You, me, your men, we kill some more, yes?"

The puzzle pieces were still drifting, not completely together. They had something urgent to do. Something about the Light Brigade.

Samuel looked at Padraig. "Corporal, please help me outside to . . ."

When Padraig assisted him to his feet, Samuel wavered briefly, but his thoughts steadied. Outside, Padraig hugged him.

"Jazus, you gave me a right fright. Are you sure you feel better?"

"Yes. It's amazing how remembering who I am steadied me."

"Good. But time flew while you were snoozing. It's after nine already, and we must get through to the allied lines. We must warn the Light Brigade. Frarat's men report that the Russian infantry is hiding in the low ground west of here while Cossacks are exposing themselves on the ridge. It's a classic trick to draw our cavalry on."

That was it . . . He'd feared a trap. More memories flooded back, and Samuel finished urinating with a sigh. Pain stabbed through his head, and he grabbed Padraig to steady himself.

Padraig's eyebrows scrunched together. "Easy. You really all right?"

"Y-yes. You're right—we must get going." The pain eased as he headed to the door, and all eyes turned to him when he entered the cottage. "Pack up, lads. We must press on. The Russians have set an ambush for the Light Brigade. We must break through the enemy line and warn them no matter what."

Lillingston's face turned ashen, and he said, "Are you insane? The valley north of the river is packed with Russians, and the hills are crawling with Cossack cavalry. We won't get twenty yards. You can't go. I forbid it."

CHAPTER TEN

September 19, 1854, morning

Pain still pulsed in Samuel's head an hour later, and his muscles screamed for rest, but his mind kept scrabbling. He was stuck in a Tartar cottage with thousands of Russians between him and the allied army. Worse, the Russians were luring his comrades into a deadly ambush. Scattered thoughts flitted through his addled brain, and reaching for one was like grasping smoke. He was weak and battered, and even if he could gather himself, a senior officer had ordered him to stay put. Giray had just parted ways with them and fled to hide out in the hills; he didn't fancy the lancers' chances of getting back to the allies. Best of luck to him; they wouldn't have made it that far without his help.

His men fidgeted around the cottage in sullen silence, save for Begley and new ally Frarat, who were feeding the horses in the barn. The old Tartar, one of Frarat's clan, was chopping rotten cabbage at the table, while Colonel Lillingston sat glaring into the fire. The odors weren't any better with the addition of the foul alcohol the Tartar was swilling. It was a wonder he could still stand. And why would a Muslim who appeared devout be drinking? Samuel remembered Giray's foul bread alcohol; apparently Giray wasn't the only one who bent the rules.

Samuel covered his face with both hands and expelled an audible breath. He'd sworn to deliver his men from their plight and had failed miserably. Perhaps his classmates had been right all along. He was a Protestant like them, true, and Anglo-Irish, like Lord Lucan and Colonel Lawrence. But he wasn't their equal.

He twisted the ragged blanket in his hand and wrestled with the ache in his head. He'd led his men that far, hadn't he? He'd fought and won every skirmish against overwhelming odds since being cut adrift a lifetime ago without losing a single man. No, he wasn't a man like Lillingston or Maxwell, cowardly entitled men. He wasn't like those bumblers Lucan and Cardigan. He was better.

Ignoring his pain, he hoisted his feet over the edge of the cot. He'd made an oath to bring his men home, and he damned well would do it, and woe betide anybody who tried to stop him —Lillingston, Maxwell, or the bloody Russians.

His shoulders were sore, lice bites stung his skin all over, his muscles ached, and his head throbbed, but he was fired up. He picked up his Colt to load it.

Padraig jumped off his stool. "What are you doing, uh, sir?"

Samuel immediately switched to Spanish. "Listen. We're going to stop this ambush and get our intelligence back to headquarters."

"And what about his lordship there?" Padraig's eyes flicked toward Lillingston. "He's given you a direct order."

"He can go to hell for all I care. How are Kiely and Hoffman? Can they ride?" Samuel half cocked the revolver and poured a measure of powder into a chamber.

"The rest has helped somewhat. Hoffman's strong, but Kiely's shoulder wound is very red, and Begley fears it's infected. He needs a doctor. They're both sleeping now."

"Rouse them." Samuel switched to English as he rammed a ball home in the chamber. "Sergeant Major, please help Begley saddle the horses." He turned the cylinder and poured powder into the next chamber.

"What do you mean?" Lillingston swept his arms through the air. "I ordered you to remain here. It's safer to wait for our army to reach us."

"Sorry, Colonel, but I won't let the Light Brigade walk into an ambush." Samuel rammed another ball home.

"You don't know for certain that the enemy is planning an ambush. I insist your men protect me until our troops arrive."

"If they arrive, sir." Samuel holstered the loaded Colt and picked up his whetstone. "I must warn them and tell them they can outflank the Russians by climbing the coastal cliffs."

"You will stay here, Lieutenant, and that's a direct order," Lillingston snarled. "If you disobey me, I'll have you up on charges."

"No, Colonel." Samuel hurled down his whetstone. "I know your type, strutting around Hyde Park and posing in the London clubs, sucking on cigars, swilling brandy, and pontificating about honor and duty. But when the war drums roll, you skulk to safe posts behind a general's coattails and far from the front line. You, sir, are a coward."

Lillingston's cheeks flushed, and he jumped to his feet. Hoffman covered his mouth with his palm, and Kiely's mouth dropped open, both men staring in disbelief. A lancer who addressed a superior in such a manner risked a flogging.

"Last chance to do what duty really calls for, Colonel. Will you ride with us?" Samuel rose and strapped on his belt.

Shaking his head, Lillingston dropped his chin to his chest and sniffled. "I won't forget this, Lieutenant."

Padraig busied himself collecting his weapons.

Samuel scanned the floor for his sharpening stone. He'd been harsh, but Lillingston had pushed him to it. "Help Kiely to the stable, Padraig. I'll take Hoffman. Come along, boys. We're returning to the regiment."

He prayed he'd sounded more confident than he felt.

What he felt was that they had no chance at all. They would all die out there within a carbine shot of the regiment, but they'd die performing their duty.

CHAPTER ELEVEN

September 19, 1854, late morning

The sun was up—hazy red—the day was blistering hot compared to the icy night, and the air was foul with smoke and horse dung. The Russians must have been confident of victory, because they hadn't yet scorched Bulganak. Samuel studied the sky in silence while the others once again donned their Cossack greatcoats and lice-infested sheepskin hats. Vultures wheeled above them on outstretched wings, soaring effortlessly and no doubt waiting to feed on the cholera bodies littering the fields in the wake of the allied army. When an army marched, the carrion gorged—both the animals and aristocratic carrion like Lord Cardigan—while ordinary soldiers marched on empty bellies and drank water from muddy puddles. He was glad Giray had said his goodbyes and slipped away. Unlike the men of Frarat's band, the Tartar trader was no warrior, and he'd suffered enough.

Frarat waddled over and patted Goldie's yellow neck. She nickered and tossed her silver mane. "Well, my friend, it's pity we won't be killing Russians together, but not you worry. Me and my men, we kill plenty."

"Where will you go?" Samuel shook the calloused paw the man extended as Tiny barked and ran circles around them.

"East to slip around the Russian flank at Kourgane Hill, then go south behind their lines." His brown eyes sparkled above his fat cheeks, and his voice rumbled. "We nip at their heels while they're fighting you."

"Ready, sir." Wagner swung into his saddle.

The rap of hooves sounded in the distance, and Samuel's pulse quickened as he stood in the stirrups to peer around the ragged hedgerow.

The hoofbeats quickly grew louder, and four Tartars galloped into the yard. They reined their lathered mounts around, the beasts prancing wildly.

A youth with hollow cheeks pointed toward the hedgerow and beyond and shouted in Russian.

"They're coming. The Cossacks coming." Frarat shouted.

They'd left it too late. Samuel undid his holster flap and drew his Colt. "Steady, lads. They won't capture us." He wouldn't give them the satisfaction of executing him.

"And here we go again." Padraig fell in beside Samuel.

The thunder of hooves drowned the clicks of the Colts' cocking hammers, and twenty Cossacks swerved around the hedgerow, a wave of steel and flesh under a thicket of lances, snarling faces, and the wild eyes of their horses rolling back in their heads. They screamed like a hundred as they couched their lances. They were only twenty yards away, their horses huffing and mud flying from their hooves.

"Fire!" Samuel pulled the trigger, glimpsing Orlov in the pack just after he fired. But the colonel vanished when a deafening volley crashed out and smoke billowed back into his face. Samuel fired as fast as he could, pumping bullets into the rearing mass of flesh, deafened by the guns blasting beside him.

The lead horses stumbled and skidded through the mud on folded knees, with horsemen catapulting over their heads. The piercing screams of men and horses filled the yard as plunging and rearing horses surged around the lancers.

His Colt was empty, a dead weight in his hand. He should have counted shots.

Samuel drew his saber as Goldie jinked to avoid a charging horse and snapped at its neck as her rider lowered his lance. The beast cried pitifully, jerking back, and Samuel chopped into the Cossack's neck. His arm jolted, then swung through, and the Cossack's shriek halted. Blood erupted from the falling body, and the severed head bounced off the horse's rump.

The fight became a melee—swords and sabers ringing, men cursing, horses whirling—and Samuel was in his element. He thrust at one man's chest, ducked his opponent's sweeping sword, and his blade locked in muscle and bone, almost dragging him off Goldie as she surged past. He freed his saber, warded off a striking shashka, and split the Cossack's head open with a savage stroke. Another poked at him with a lance. Samuel hammered it aside with the Colt in his left hand and hacked the man's arm to the bone. The screeching Cossack swerved past Samuel.

"I've got him. Death or glory!" Padraig stood in his stirrups and slashed down to shatter the Cossack's skull.

Kiely hollered, and Samuel wheeled on Goldie. Across the yard, Orlov, his face twisted with hate, yanked his saber out of Kiely's neck and craned around as Frarat pulled the last mounted Cossack from his saddle and followed him to the ground. Orlov mouthed a curse, sawed his reins, and raked his horse with spurs. The horse reared, its eyes rolling to white, and galloped from the yard.

If Orlov escaped, he'd raise the alarm. Energy pulsed through Samuel. Save for Padraig, his men were on foot now, battling the last standing Cossacks. All but Kiely, who lay unmoving on the ground. "Padraig, we must stop him. Come on, Goldie."

Her coat lathered in sweat, Goldie leaped into a canter and then stretched into a gallop. Her powerful muscles flexed under

Samuel's knees as she thundered into the lane, and he bent over her mane to help her speed. She swayed around the corner, hooves slithering for traction, and sped up. But Orlov was already thirty yards ahead, with mud spurting up from his stallion's racing hooves.

Samuel's throat tightened. Goldie was a thoroughbred with heart, and she might have caught Orlov's stallion if she was fit. But weeks of confinement at sea and eating badly had stressed her—she was far from her best. Hoofbeats thumped behind him. Padraig.

Samuel could have shot at Orlov at thirty yards, but his Colt was empty, and he couldn't risk the carbine's single shot. Now it was up to Goldie. He needed her to dig deep and catch Orlov, even if it destroyed her. Hundreds of lives depended on Samuel warning the Light Brigade.

CHAPTER TWELVE

September 19, 1854, late morning

Goldie was magnificent. The hedgerows flashed past as she extended out, and mud flicked up from her hooves as she soared down the long lane. Samuel rose and fell to the rhythm of her heaving breaths, melding with her, a partner in this race for the lives of many. Pain stabbed his head each time her feet jarred down, and soon he was dizzy, but he couldn't slow. He'd no idea where they were—somewhere outside the village of Bulganak. He'd been unconscious when they took him to the cottage. Padraig knew more, but the hoofbeats were dwindling behind Samuel. Few cavalry mounts had the stamina of Goldie or of Orlov's black stallion.

A glimpse of the coastal road flashed through a gap in the trees—only two hundred yards away. He had to stop Orlov before then, but Goldie was flagging. Poor girl was giving her all, her nostrils flaring in time with her labored breath, but yellow foam lathered her neck and flanks. Ahead of them, Orlov's horse ran strongly, widening the gap. Should he risk the carbine?

He rounded another bend and ducked to avoid a low-hanging

branch. Orlov was seventy yards ahead, almost at the coastal road. Goldie stumbled. The chase was too much for her. Now he had no choice.

He reined in. "Whoa! Whoa, Goldie."

He dropped the saber and had the rifle in hand before Goldie halted. He swung down and cocked the hammer. He fought to slow his wheezing breath and aimed at Orlov, who was almost at the junction. His head was woozy, and his vision blurred. He blinked rapidly and closed his weaker eye.

Steady, steady. He must control his quivering body; he'd have only one shot. One chance. He risked missing Orlov at that range; he'd have to hit the horse. He sighted, his finger hovering over the trigger, and the smooth stock cold against his cheek.

Holding a breath, he aimed at the shrinking hindquarter—a scanty target already—and pulled the trigger. The carbine barked, kicking hard against his shoulder, and smoke obscured his vision. The pungent smoke blew past him, and through the vanishing haze he watched the stallion stagger and fall. Orlov kicked free of the stirrups, seemed to float for seconds, and tumbled as he landed. He rolled through the muck and then lay supine.

Samuel snatched up his saber and mounted, and Goldie was cantering before he swung his foot over her back. Orlov sprang up, covered in mud, and reached for the pistol in his belt. He would hit Samuel for sure, knock him clean out of the saddle. Samuel tucked in his elbows, making himself as small as possible.

Orlov stepped into a wide stance, rigid as a lance. He had lost his shako, and mud caked his dirty yellow hair and his face. He sighted his pistol, and icy fingers pattered down Samuel's back. He could wheel and flee now, save his life. Perhaps they would only be taken prisoner, not shot. His men would live. He would live. His pushed back his fear with a shiver.

Goldie was at full gallop, with Samuel's seat rising and falling to the rhythm of her labored breaths. Leather creaked and tack jangled as she pounded down on Orlov. Pounded down on death.

Samuel squeezed the hilt of his saber so tightly, his fingers numbed. He remembered a fifteen-year-old boy staring down the barrel of a dueling pistol at fifteen paces—facing another bully in a very different time—and he hadn't flinched then. He tensed. He wouldn't flinch now. Too many men would die if he failed.

At twenty yards the pistol's muzzle looked like the mouth of a cannon. Orlov's face twisted with hate, and his lips drew back in a snarl. Samuel imagined he could hear the man's hellish howl.

Now!

Samuel slid down Goldie's left side as Jerry had taught him years before, and the pistol barked. Clinging like a limpet to Goldie's neck—face pressed against her wet neck, smelling the sweat of her effort—Samuel felt nothing, and Goldie didn't break a stride.

Orlov had missed both of them. Samuel heaved himself upright.

Smoke drifted clear, and ten yards away Orlov threw down the pistol and drew his saber with a curse. Samuel swung his blade to right engage. He had him. He'd ride the murderous bastard down.

Unwavering and confident, Orlov straddled the middle of the road with his blade held before him.

Samuel lashed out, aiming for Orlov's neck, and missed— Orlov had ducked. The Russian bastard had timed his move as deftly as Samuel had. Goldie ran for a few yards, and as Samuel wheeled her, he glimpsed several hussars on the main road. If they heard the pistol shot, they were already riding to investigate. He swung down from the saddle.

Orlov hefted his blade, his eyes wide, the right one icy and glaring at Samuel, the lazy one staring into the meadow. He swatted the air with his saber almost playfully—if anyone could believe that cold-hearted bastard could be impish.

"Aha, the young lancer's a gentleman of honor and won't ride down his opponent." He spat toward Samuel. "Damn your honor, boy. You killed some of my finest warriors and made a fool of me. I'm going to cut you to pieces, take you apart limb by limb just as you did those gunners." He whipped his saber in a dazzling circle, and the blade whistled death.

Up close, Orlov was shorter than Samuel but stockier, and that extra weight was muscle. His enormous nose was flattened, and the purple scar through his thin lips marked him as a duelist. The man would know how to fight.

Samuel advanced silently to meet him, his head hammering painfully, sweat pouring down his back and sides.

"Your situation's hopeless, boy. Even if you beat me—most unlikely—my men are scouring the valleys for you. They know you're trapped between the rivers. Pinned between two Russian armies."

"Perhaps they'll find me, but you'll be dead." Samuel watched Orlov's eyes for a signal, but that lazy eye floating about was disconcerting. *Misleading.* He'd ignore it and watch the right eye.

Orlov spat. "Dead? Do you know many men I've killed in duels, famous fencers renowned all over our magnificent empire?" He sprang up on his toes and slashed the air with his blade.

Someone shouted in the distance; the hussars were coming. Samuel's nerves jangled. He had to end this quickly and lead the hussars away from the others. "Going to fight me with your beak, Orlov? Bore me to death with fantastic claims? I'd bet my life you weary your opponents until they fall on your sword just to escape your prattle."

Orlov shifted, the one eye fixed on Samuel, and then reached out his saber to touch Samuel's blade. He stood loose, but from shoulder to the tip of his blade he was hard and as unyielding as a spear. He lunged, his blade flicking out faster than a serpent's tongue. Samuel skipped back and blocked him.

Orlov danced a step forward, and his saber sliced toward Samuel's side. Samuel parried, the blades rang together, and Samuel disengaged. The Russian sneered and slashed at Samuel's neck, his blade a blur. Samuel again blocked.

Orlov stepped closer, Samuel retreated. Orlov's attacks came like lightning, his blade everywhere—twinkling, darting, testing. They shuffled back and forth on the muddy road, sabers singing and clashing, exchanging hard blows that sent shocks up Samuel's arm. There was no traction in the thick mud. It was like fencing on ice.

Another shout declared that the hussars drew near. Blood pulsed in Samuel's ears. *Finish this.* He thrust at Orlov's thigh, but Orlov parried and countered with rapid-fire cuts, left and right, almost slicing through Samuel's guard. When Orlov lunged at his groin, Samuel skipped back, slipped in the cursed mud, and lost his balance. Orlov pounced, chopping down as Samuel landed on one knee, and Samuel scarcely raised his saber in time. The blow jolted his arm, shoulder, and spine.

Orlov leaped back with a flourish of his saber. "Cat can't kill his mouse too soon; we'll play some more."

Samuel got to his feet and rubbed his muddy hand down his trousers. He was better than this. He'd trained with swords since he could first walk, and the only man who could match him was Padraig.

Where was Padraig? He'd heard a horse follow him out of the yard.

"Come now, Lieutenant, are you giving up? Not good enough? Better fight, boy, because this contest is to the death." Orlov stamped forward, his saber hissing. His blade darted everywhere and then licked out and froze between them at the end of his extended arm. "Do you hear riders coming? Yours or mine, I wonder. We'd best finish this duel either way."

Samuel shook his head to clear the dizziness. He attacked, cutting, thrusting, and warding with a blistering sequence, trying every move he'd practiced over the years. Orlov's scarred lips pressed together, and he retreated before the flickering blade.

Samuel whirled his saber around Orlov's and then a second time before with a change of direction he flicked the Russian's blade out of his hand. He shouted with relief and triumph and plunged his saber through Orlov's breast even as Orlov's saber flew over his shoulder.

Orlov folded forward, and his eyes dulled as a blast of his garlic-tainted breath washed over Samuel. He collapsed without uttering a sound.

Samuel pulled his saber free with a grunt, and a last breath hissed from Orlov's lips. He spun around and looked up the lane. Five hussars halted at the laneway with their black frock coats billowing behind them, the sunlight bright on their gold trim. Samuel's head spun, and his legs turned to jelly. He recognized the uniform from his studies at Sandhurst—Kievsky Hussars. Russia's finest cavalrymen.

He could never defeat five of them.

CHAPTER THIRTEEN

September 19, 1854, late morning

Goldie, blowing hard, stood splay-legged, her golden coat lathered with sweat. She could never outrun them. Samuel rammed his saber into the mud and pulled out his powder horn. The hussars shouted and spurred their mounts into the lane.

He jammed a ball into the chamber, rotated the cylinder, and rammed the ball down with the loading lever. The ground trembled, and the drum of hooves grew closer. No time to look. His hand trembled as he turned the cylinder and loaded a second chamber.

The thunder of hooves and the horses' heaving breaths were too close. No time for another load.

He fitted percussion caps, expecting a saber to hack into his neck, and cocked the hammer as a shadow reared above him. Throwing up his arm, he fired blindly.

The bullet hit the hussar's chest and plucked him from the saddle. The next rider swerved around the falling body as the stricken hussar screamed. A third rider charged in, leaning over his horse's neck with saber extended.

Gasping for breath, Samuel shot that third rider in the throat. He plucked his standing saber from the mud and threw himself into the ditch. His Colt was empty again.

The last two hussars thundered past, and the wind of a sweeping blade stirred his hair. They cursed, wheeling their prancing horses with the third rider, and roared at each other, while a fallen hussar writhed and cried two feet from Samuel. He caught the bitter scent of the hussar's urine.

This was it; he was out of luck, both good and bad. Thorns clawed his tunic as he rolled out of the bush and stood to face the three hussars, bloody saber held across his chest and fused to his hand. He was a dead man, but he'd sell his life dearly in the hope he'd maul them before they went after his men.

Sabers flashed in the morning sun, the bellowing hussars raked spurs to their horses, and they leaped forward, muzzles flaring. A gun boomed. One hussar threw his arms high and tumbled over the rump of his charging horse.

The revolver barked twice more, and another hussar danced like a marionette before collapsing sideways off his horse. Samuel dived into the ditch again and huffed hard as the hussar horses galloped past, splattering him with mud. He rolled to his knees to watch them. The last hussar swayed in the saddle, and his saber scribbled in the air until he fell from his horse twenty yards away. The fleeing mare shuddered to a violent stop, its reins tangled in the dead man's hand.

Still on his knees, Samuel jerked around.

Padraig stood panting in the middle of the road, smoke drifting around the Colt in his hand. "Sure and I can't leave you alone for a second, can I?"

Samuel slumped back on his heels, drained. "Could you have timed it tighter?"

"What kind of gratitude is that? I've been shooting men to save your arse since I was fifteen. You hurt?"

"N-no. Just shaken. Damnation, what a mess. They're all

dead, and the poor stallion. We have to put him out of his misery."

Goldie plodded over and nuzzled Samuel as he climbed unsteadily to his feet to pet her. "Sweet Goldie, what would I do without you? Ran your big heart out, old girl, didn't you?" He nuzzled her, the coat soft yet spiky on his cheek. "I'm going to find you a big apple when we get back to camp."

Bloodied bodies lay sprawled around the lane, and the black stallion thrashed and whinnied pitifully, its hind quarters twisted. The hussars' horses would have been fresher than their own, but three had stampeded onto the coast road. Samuel hurried to free the horse tangled in the dead man's reins, and a pistol barked behind him, silencing the stallion.

"One horse ran toward the cottage. Goldie's played out, so I'll ride this mare and she can follow us." Samuel led the mare over to Orlov's corpse and stooped to search him.

"Bloody antique." Padraig tossed aside the pistol he'd plucked from a hussar's holster and began reloading his Colt. "We better get back and see what happened. At least all of our lads survived the fight."

Samuel's vision blurred. "Not Kiely. This Russian bastard killed the poor lad." Why was it always the young and innocent who fell first?

"What did you say, Kiely? No way. Never." Padraig stopped reloading and gaped at Samuel. "Are you sure? Be—"

"I'm not blind." Samuel expelled a breath. "I'm sorry. He was just a boy. How many more will die before we get back?" *If* they got back. But he wouldn't say that, not even to Padraig. They were going to make it back to the regiment.

He checked another of the Russian's pockets—a purse with a few gold and silver coins. He'd give them to the old Tartar, meager payment for the trouble they'd brought to his home. The only other item of interest was the oilskin package in Orlov's breast pocket, which Samuel shoved deep into his own trouser pocket. "What happened to you back there? You were just behind me."

"They shot my horse in the melee, and he collapsed a ways back."

"Glad you could make it. Ride the mare. I'll take Goldie." Samuel reloaded his Colt, and every muscle complained as he heaved himself into the saddle.

Gunfire echoed as they trotted back to the cottage, and Samuel straightened in the saddle. They were still fighting back there. He palmed his Colt and urged Goldie into a labored gallop.

They turned into the yard, Samuel bending low over Goldie's neck. Fallen men and horses littered the earth, and one Cossack squatted against the stable wall, staring sightlessly at the pink intestines—teeming with flies—that had spilled out in front of him. Samuel was shocked to see his eyes blink. Goldie was a warhorse, but even she balked at the stench of blood, shit, and vomit. She skittered sideways, and Samuel swung down, his skin crawling.

Wagner stood over a dead horse, a smoking pistol still extended. Begley was crouching beside Kiely's bloody body, and Price was helping Frarat carry a dead Tartar into the adjacent field.

Samuel holstered his gun and ran to Wagner. "He's dead?"

Wagner sniffed and wiped his nose. "Ja. Poor lad. And him so far from home."

Samuel had never seen the noncommissioned officer show such emotion before, and tears welled behind his eyelids. "I got the bastard who killed him, but that's little consolation. Poor Kiely. We'll give him a proper burial before we move on, but we must be quick; Russians are everywhere. Begley, pick the best Cossack horses and round them up with Price; ours are spent. I'll ride that bay; it belonged to one of the hussars we fought up the road." He checked his watch. Ten fifteen. The Russkies expected the allies to reach their ambush point in the afternoon.

Wagner was looking at him, eyes widening. "You killed more Russians?"

"You'll see soon enough." Samuel headed to the stable for a spade. "Let's get moving. We're running out of time."

Frarat and the youth with hollowed cheeks who'd ridden in to warn that the Cossacks were coming were the only Tartars to survive the fight in the yard, and they had slaughtered all the injured Cossacks in their grief, all except the gutted one against the wall. They'd probably left him to suffer a slow death. That cruelty turned Samuel's stomach, but there was nothing he could do about it now. He ripped a greatcoat from one of the dead Cossacks and placed it over the wounded man's chest with a sympathetic smile and held a canteen to the man's lips. The Cossack groaned, and the light left his eyes. Samuel rose unsteadily against the weight of sleepless nights, his pounding head, and the deaths of the many men whose lives he'd just taken. There was no glory in this part of war, just death. No matter what the regiment's war cry proclaimed.

They buried Kiely, marked his grave with a crude cross, and Samuel felt deflated in body and mind as he prayed over him. The boy had been his responsibility, and he'd failed him. Afterward, they helped Frarat bury his comrades in a single grave and marked it with a pile of stones.

The big Tartar insisted on joining their dash through the Russian lines; he was keen to kill more infidels, almost as eager as the boy with hollow cheeks. They donned their Cossack greatcoats and foul sheepskin hats—now bloodied as well as teeming with creatures—over their uniforms. All except Samuel and Frarat would carry lances to complete their disguises. Samuel wore the sable cloak again to cover the carbine hanging from his saddle. Guns like that were a rare find in a Russian army which still used muskets. He had no plans to give himself away.

He had no plans to lose any other men.

CHAPTER FOURTEEN

September 19, 1854, midday

The noon sun was blistering hot, and steam drifted from the mud when they set out. Goldie latched onto the bay mare's rump as if she resented her for stealing Samuel.

There was little traffic on the coast road. All the troops must have been in position and hunkered down to spring their trap on the Light Brigade. At that thought, Samuel urged the bay into a canter. There was no time to waste, but they didn't need to attract undue attention either. He reined the bay back to a trot and reflexively clenched and unclenched his fingers, trying to ease their ache.

Padraig rested his hands on his saddle and nodded at Begley. "Why the dour face? It was only a dog."

"Yes, but it was a fine dog. I was going to take him back to England."

Price chuckled. "Fat chance of that. If the quartermaster had seen it, he'd have thrown a saddle on it and given it to a lancer."

Begley cursed under his breath. "Not a chance. He was mine, the spoils of war."

"That bloody dog was far too classy for the likes of you," Padraig said. "He raced back to headquarters, knowing he's safer hiding behind his general's skirts with the other cowardly toffs than charging an infantry line with us."

Samuel attacked his flea bites with vigor. There had been no time to wash; his skin crawled and his eyes were gritty. "We're not charging anyone, Corporal. We're bluffing our way through. We're Cossack scouts sent by General Menshikov to reconnoiter the allied advance, and that's what Frarat will tell anyone who stops us."

The land wasn't unlike West Cork, with rolling green meadows and cornfields. The air smelled of grass, wild thyme, and baking mud. He pictured autumn back home in Clonakilty, the dormant pastures of undulating countryside unfurling mile after fertile mile, flat stone walls dividing them into a deranged quilt, and the trees fluttering copper and gold in the waning sun. Samuel sat straighter in the saddle. They were going to make it back to the regiment, and someday he'd return to Clonakilty.

They rode past a few stragglers in brown or gray greatcoats, ragged emaciated men lugging ancient muskets, but nobody paid them much attention.

Creaks and moans sounded ahead, and hands flew to the comfort of the Colts inside their greatcoats.

"Steady, lads. No weapons." The moans rose and fell but never stopped, and Samuel cocked his head to better listen.

Moments later, the fetor from three carts trundling toward them churned his stomach. The worst of the foul odors was rotting flesh. Samuel wasn't the only one to gag.

What first looked like a pile of bodies on the carts materialized into soldiers packed like slaves on a slave ship, wretches shaking with fever, seeping blood from dysentery, or gagging on their own vomit. One man rolled out and flopped like a fish in the mud, struggling for breath, drenched in sweat or other fluids. He feebly lifted an arm with skin blistered raw, but the carts wobbled on, hell on wheels, and nobody spared him a glance.

Dropping his gaze to the ground, Samuel heeled the bay past the carts and around the suffering man, blinking as the scene conjured nightmare memories of Ireland's famine.

The starving and sick had sprawled listlessly in the muddy hedgerows of West Cork, dressed in soiled rags or barely anything at all, and blue with the cold or white with fever, most barefooted—the scraps and remnants of humanity. Those with the strength stumbled to their feet calling to Samuel for food, while others lay in the mud and called out weakly, begging Father Lyons for a blessing to send them to the grave.

Anglo-Irish aristocrats, men like Lucan and Lawrence, had sinned against Ireland, and some day they'd pay for their sins. He drew back his shoulders. But now he had to see his men to safety. He heeled the mare into a trot, and wringing their reins and gagging, the others followed.

Price lowered the collar he'd been holding to his nose. "And I thought the British army bad. I'll take old Bloodyback any d—"

"Hold your whist," Padraig hissed. "Do you want to draw the Russkies down on us?"

Samuel willed his toes to uncurl. "Nobody speaks until we're through their lines."

Farmland gave way to a forest as they rode uphill, and Frarat dropped back. "There's valley ahead and another hill. They'll hide in the valley, wait for the allies to ride over. Then it get interesting, no?"

Interesting? How about terrifying, you bloodthirsty old goat. "Thank you, Frarat." Samuel dropped back to the others. "Right, lads. Keep moving and eyes forward no matter what you see. This is the last mile—don't falter now. Hoffman, how are you bearing up?"

Hoffman was colorless, and his stringy hair was plastered back from his forehead. He rubbed the scar on his nose, a common habit. "Right as rain, sir, and looking forward to a bumper of gin."

"Bumper, hah!" Price said. "You'll be lucky to find a teaspoon full."

The bay crested the ridge, and Samuel jerked upright in the saddle. The shallow valley three miles long and half a mile broad was covered with cornfields and orchards and thousands of Russians crouching behind a low fresh-dug dike. Their dull uniforms blended into the earth; only the sun's glint on the bayonets and badges of the few men standing gave them away. They'd concealed a dozen artillery pieces behind piles of brush. From his position, Samuel could see them clearly, but the Light Brigade would not. Behind the line, two thousand cavalrymen stood beside their horses, ready to mount when they sprang the trap.

Beyond the massed army, a hundred Cossacks sat their horses on the hilltop.

The bait.

Samuel's breath hitched, and he reined in the mare. It was going to be touch and go to pass that horde unchallenged.

"Lucifer's boots." Padraig's eyes were bulging. "I've never seen so many soldiers before. How will we get by?"

Samuel had been through too much to stop now. "We'll ride straight through like we own the place. We're bloody Cossacks." Samuel heeled his horse into a trot.

He suppressed the urge to rub the tic under his left eye. Suppressed, too, the urge to turn and flee. There was nowhere to run—Russians surrounded them. Perhaps they should have returned to the coast after all. Perhaps . . .

Enough! He'd made a plan, and he would stick to it.

The sable cloak was hot and heavy when he rolled his shoulders. Sweat streamed down his back, stinging his flea-bitten flesh. Reminding him he was still alive to feel the nasty bites.

He forced himself to smile—a proud Cossack excited to take on the oh-so-vaunted allied expedition come to challenge him in his own land. Come to tell him and his people what they could and could not do.

They were twenty yards from the last lines of Russians hunkered on the ground. Gaunt men with black beards or mustaches—bored, hungry, and fidgeting—followed the *Cossacks* with tired eyes. Did they recognize that they were Westerners? Did they suspect?

Vultures soared in the brassy sky, wheeling as gracefully as eagles on their white-tipped wings. Harbingers of death. They knew that when armies marched, they would soon feed. Samuel spat out the saliva flooding his mouth.

A man shouted from the field south of the road, and Samuel shifted only his eyes, never turning his head. He'd keep riding, pretending he'd heard nothing.

A major wearing a white cross belt over his blue tunic, mud-splattered white trousers, and a bronze helmet with a crowned eagle on top strode quickly over. Two soldiers, holding muskets across their chests, followed him.

Beneath his cloak, Samuel closed his hand around Kiely's Colt in his belt.

The officer jabbered again, closer, his voice harsh and demanding. Samuel cocked the hammer and fought to steady his breathing. His headache was back, pounding worse than ever. Frarat wheeled his horse and rode over to the officer as the British lancers shifted in their saddles. Hoffman, deathly pale, groaned and swayed. The damned man had better keep his arse on the horse.

The officer and Frarat argued, words flying in bursts like rolling musket fire, the pitch and tone of their voices rising. Then Frarat laughed—a deep boom rising from his belly—and slapped his knee. The officer threw back his head and laughed along with him. They shook hands, Frarat stood in his stirrups, plucked an apple from the branch above him, and tossed it to the officer.

He picked another for himself, took a huge bite, and cantered back to the others on the road. "It's fine, but don't look at him. Keep riding."

Blue hussars lurked in the orchards on the south side, close to the rise of the ridge, watching the lancers. Samuel couldn't see the tail of the horde, but there were hundreds of them, and on the right stood gray hussars and Cossacks. Samuel's breaths came shallow. Madness had led him to believe they'd get away with this, but there were too many of them and all watching the strange band trotting between their ranks. Any moment now an officer must stop them. *Get on with it, Frarat.*

It was almost as if Frarat had heard Samuel's fervent wish— he tapped his spurs to his mount's flanks, and she launched into a canter. Samuel fussed with his cloak, rearranging it over his lancer's tunic for quick access to his Colt as he let his men speed up past him. He'd go last to make sure they made it back to the allied lines.

In a jiffy that took forever, they were past the cavalry and laboring uphill toward the throng of Cossacks on the ridge— Ural warriors in black mink hats and greatcoats, and fur-wrapped Kubanians from the Black Sea with their stringy, wide-brimmed bonnets pulled down over their brows. Beneath his cloak, Samuel drew Kiely's Colt from his belt. If they didn't believe Frarat was leading his men to scout the enemy, all hell was going to break loose. But they parted, black eyebrows furrowing or shooting up their foreheads as they wheeled back like opening gates, and Frarat led the lancers through.

When they reached the crest of the hill, Samuel saw the Light Brigade a half mile away dressing ranks in preparation to charge. They looked splendid—most regiments in navy blue, the Queen's Own Hussars in green, and the Cherry Pickers in their distinctive red pantaloons. Relief washed over him. His small band was going to make it.

Urgent shouts erupted from the cavalry massed behind them, and a horseman dashed from their ranks, mud flying from the hooves of his galloping horse as he raced toward them.

Samuel heeled his mare. "Ride for your lives!"

———

The lancers and Frarat smacked their mounts into a canter and then a gallop and charged down the muddy road. Samuel threw back his cloak and fired as fast as he could into the ranks of startled Cossacks, and the Cossacks' mounts skittered backward and sideways. Ahead of him, his lancers twisted in their saddles and fired, smoke billowing from their barking Colts. The mare under Samuel had heart, for she careered headlong after his men, frisking like a mountain sheep, and he clung hard with his knees as he switched Kiely's empty Colt for his own. He again craned around to look behind.

Goldie was right on the mare's flank, her head bobbing and her mane billowing like a silver pennon. The Cossacks were streaming down the hill after them, only fifty yards behind, brandishing swords or couching lances. Thank God they didn't have Colts. He fired the Colt again to deter the pursuers, then faced the road ahead. It was better to concentrate on reaching the shelter of the Light Brigade.

Lucan and Cardigan sat their horses in front of the brigade; it looked like they were bickering again. Useless lumps. One of these days their vanity and arrogance might be the death of the cavalry brigades. The mare's lungs were pumping like a bellows, froth spewing back from her muzzle as she raced flat out. The others were holding their own ahead, even Hoffman, who was swaying but holding on. Two hundred yards ahead, Lucan wheeled away from Cardigan, and both men drew sabers.

They thought his men were part of a Cossack charge. He fumbled with the binding on his cloak and threw it off to reveal his lancer's uniform, roaring with all his might, "Hold up, don't charge."

The line opened and Samuel's men spilled through, screaming at the lancers to stand fast but open fire. The Cossacks were ninety yards away, horse hooves drumming the turf, sunlight flashing on their blades.

Lucan was fingering the base of his neck and frowning stupidly, but Cardigan was raising his saber to call for a charge.

Samuel reined in the mare between them. "It's a trap. There are thousands more beyond the hill. We were betrayed. Hold the line and fire at those Cossacks; the Colts will stop them."

"Stand your ground and fire at will. That's an order." The booming voice of authority came from behind Lucan.

Revolvers crashed like rolling thunder, and chains of smoke erupted from the British line. Samuel wheeled as several Cossacks tumbled from their saddles, and a handful of horses pitched over. The charge seemed to hit a wall, and in an eye blink the enemy was in confusion, with horses rearing and dancing. The Cossacks turned and raced back up the hill.

"A cess on your hide, who gave that order?" Lucan snarled and turned his horse to face the brigade.

"*I* did." General Airey cantered out from the ranks on a gray stallion, trailed by his aides-de-camp. While at Sandhurst, Samuel had heard a guest lecture from Lord Raglan's Quartermaster-General. Airey was in his midfifties, a lean man with white sideburns and weary eyes. "We can't risk a charge. What if the lieutenant's right?"

Lucan scowled. "Pah! This man's nothing but a blackguard, a known troublemaker back in Ireland. We can't trust him."

Samuel fisted both hands. What did Lucan mean? "We just came from behind enemy lines, sir," he said to Airey. "They've set a trap for the Light Brigade. Two thousand horsemen, backed by six thousand infantry, wait behind that ridge. We've been betrayed, sir."

"Betrayed?" Lucan turned his back on Samuel. "Poppycock. This man's a menace, sir."

Airey frowned at Samuel. "Who betrayed us, Lieutenant?"

"One of your staff officers, General. Captain Maxwell."

A storm of gasps and muttering crackled through the ranks, and the aides behind Airey separated to expose Maxwell's heated face.

"Captain Maxwell, come here, if you please." Airy didn't even look back.

Maxwell walked his horse forward, averting his eyes from Samuel.

"My corporal saw him signaling the shore back in Varna and dismissed it, thinking he was saying goodbye to a girl or something. But when he caught Captain Maxwell signaling again in Calamita Bay, he alerted me. I was remiss in reporting the activity to my superior earlier, sir. I'm sorry." Samuel stared at the ground. A bully from his school days had intimidated him . . . However, that wouldn't happen again. He was better than any of those bastards who'd picked on him in school.

The Cossacks were holding their horses out of range, snarling and yelling from two hundred yards up the hill.

"Before I could mention anything, Captain Maxwell ordered C Company to take the last raft despite the approach of night and the worsening sea. This was on the seventeenth. Then he cut seven of us adrift, sir, hoping we'd drown, I daresay." *Let's see you bully your way out of this fix, Maxwell.*

Airey's head twisted around until he faced Maxwell. "I'm sure you can explain."

For a moment Maxwell wrestled with his tongue, and then he snarled, "Preposterous, General. These men are trying to cover—"

"Then what's this?" Samuel withdrew the oilskin package from his pocket, and Maxwell's chin quivered. "I took these notes from a Russian colonel. It's all there—General Raglan's battle plan, troop counts, and the state of our supplies . . . And written in this coward's hand." He handed the package to Airey, who promptly opened it.

"It's Maxwell's hand for certain. Why—"

All eyes were on Airey when Maxwell spurred his chestnut charger, and the beast lunged past Samuel. In a flash, Maxwell was clear of the brigade and racing toward the Cossacks.

"Stop that traitor." Airey's nostrils flared as he pointed at Maxwell, already halfway to the Cossacks.

General Brudenell shook his head. "It's too late, my lord."

Not if Samuel could help it. He lifted his carbine, aimed at Maxwell's back, and pulled the trigger. The weapon boomed and kicked, and bitter-tasting smoke blew back on him.

Maxwell reared in the saddle and crashed to the road ten feet from the Cossacks.

Samuel lowered the smoking carbine and looked at Airey. "His actions caused the death of Kiely, one of my men, sir." The generals should remember poor Kiely, the first of the British to die in combat in that war. A death that should never have happened.

"Where did you get the carbine, Kingston?" Lucan snapped. "More of your insubordination. I should—"

"You should thank the lieutenant, Lord Lucan. We all should. Were it not for him, we might be burying you on the south side of that ridge."

Samuel's lungs expanded. Such praise from a general like Airey was rare. "Thank you, sir, but I couldn't have done it without my men. They're the courageous ones. And if the general will indulge me, there's more. We've seen and noted the enemy positions south of the Alma. They're very strong, but there's a weak point."

Airey's shaggy eyebrows lifted. "Really, Lieutenant? I think you'd better ride with me to General Raglan's position." He wheeled his horse and rode back through the lancers.

A grinning Padraig rode over and gathered Goldie's reins, and Lucan expelled a derisive snort as Samuel rode after Airey.

Lucan didn't like Samuel, and unlike the case with Maxwell's hatred, Samuel couldn't fathom why. Perhaps Lucan held a grudge because Samuel's father had condemned Anglo-Irish landowners like Lucan for their cruelty and greed during the famine. Samuel would be wary of the cavalry commander.

CHAPTER FIFTEEN

September 20, 1854, morning

"The coast cliffs aren't as steep as the Russians believe, Lord Raglan." Samuel took another sip from Raglan's brandy flask. "Only a handful of men are stationed on top to defend them. I'm certain the French can scale up there and turn the enemy flank." Who would ever believe he held the attention of the overall commander of the allied forces in Crimea? A man who'd served as military secretary to the Duke of Wellington.

With a gaggle of senior officers, they stood on a knoll overlooking the muddy Alma River as it meandered through the valley. Beyond the river the wooded slopes rose gently on both sides of the redoubts, but the cleared slope below the redoubts was a killing ground.

"I see. I hope you're right." Raglan twisted the empty right sleeve of his frock coat and glanced at Airey. "Do you think he's right?"

Raglan had lost the arm in the Battle of Waterloo. *That* was significant. And now that hero of Waterloo, the man who stormed the breach at Badajoz, was listening to Samuel.

Raglan had a kindly demeanor and seemed more like a clerk than a warrior as he scratched his disheveled white hair while hemming and hawing. "The French have our right flank, so this is really Marshal Saint-Arnaud's bailiwick, and I didn't enjoy telling him what to do. Hmm . . . The French are touchy that way. Do you think he minded, General Airey?"

Samuel pursed his lips. This was the key to victory, and Raglan had asked Saint-Arnaud to assault the cliffs based on Samuel's report the day before, and now he should just let them get on with it. Yet with the French already moving into position to attack the heights behind the Alma River, Raglan was second-guessing himself. Dithering was the last thing Samuel had expected. He drank again to hide his expression. No wonder the campaign had stalled already.

Airey hadn't appeared out of sorts after Samuel shot his aide-de-camp the day before. Now he tugged at his bottom lip before telling Raglan, "I think it's a jolly fine idea, my lord. I see no reason to call it off."

Thank goodness for that, but why was Raglan not acting on Samuel's other suggestion? "If I may be so bold, Lord Raglan. Many of our men will die in this direct assault on the Russian redoubts; there are a hundred cannons up there. I implore you to consider my recommendation that the Light Brigade ride around the Russian right flank on Kourgane Hill and assault that position from the south. In that—"

Lucan muttered under his breath and stalked up to Raglan's shoulder. "A reckless idea, Kingston, and as commander of the cavalry, I couldn't support it. Our job is to scout and keep the enemy cavalry at bay, and we can't do that if we're tearing all over Crimea on the whim of a snotty lieutenant."

"I say, General Bingham, that's rather harsh." Raglan raised his eyebrows and gestured at Samuel. "The lieutenant is doing his duty, and we owe him much for saving your Light Brigade yesterday. Nevertheless, General, I'll follow your advice."

Raglan took Samuel's elbow and drew him aside. "General

Bingham's our cavalry commander, I can't undermine him. Enough of that, Lieutenant. I asked you here to thank you for your courage in saving the Light Brigade yesterday. I assure you I won't forget this. Now if you'll excuse me, I've a battle to win. I wish you the joy of the day."

Lucan was still scowling as Samuel shook Raglan's left hand awkwardly and returned to where Padraig held Goldie.

"Did he promote you? Give you a medal?" Padraig handed him Goldie's reins as she head-butted Samuel playfully.

Samuel swatted the air. "Hell, no. It's Lucan again. He disparaged everything I suggested. I don't know what that man has against me."

Padraig mounted his horse and grinned. "Maybe he thinks you're Catholic. He hates us. He had Colonel Lawrence deprive me of that fine horse we took from the Russian hussar yesterday. Lawrence saddled me with this Syrian nag instead."

Samuel shot a glance back at Lucan. "That was petty, but it never occurred to me that Lucan was behind it. But now that you mention it, I—"

"You're too trusting to see it. They're both Anglo-Irishmen, same as you, but they have it in for you. Mark my words."

Padraig's disgust at the ruling class made him overly suspicious. Samuel dismissed his doubts and checked Goldie's saddle girth. It was loose, and he pursed his lips as he cinched it tighter. She'd never been so thin. They'd given the horses no time to recover from the sea voyage, and now they were going into action again.

Five minutes later the four-mile-wide advance was an incredible sight as they rode east to rejoin the train of cavalry in the left flank. All bustle and activity with compact lines of soldiers, artillery, ammunition, horses, bullocks, packhorses, mules, and oxen.

The French marched on the right flank where the guns of the fleet protected them, and eight thousand Ottoman troops followed the French.

Padraig pointed to the Algerian Zouaves already scaling the cliff face, standing out in their blue coats and red pantaloons as they climbed. "Look there. Raglan would have been too late to stop them."

Samuel sat taller in the saddle as the British advanced, with the skirmish line of green-jacketed riflemen flitting ahead of the redcoats. "That's history for you. Nobody has seen such large armies in the field since Waterloo, and that was almost forty years ago."

"And there's never been such an idiotic reason to gather them," Padraig said.

"What do you mean?"

"What's this war about? Tsar Nicholas says it's religion." Padraig waved one hand. "*Rubbish*. And what's our excuse? We don't have a good one. We're here because the aristocrats want to protect their precious investments in India. And when Russia threatened the Black Sea, the greedy lords rattled their sabers and the stupid public jumped on the wagon. Now those same people are baying for Russian blood, but those bastards are sitting down to their rashers and eggs at home while we're out here facing the music."

Samuel knew better than to argue when Padraig began his rants. "Speaking about music, I wish the Russians would punch holes in those highlander bagpipes. What an infernal racket they make."

Padraig chuckled.

"What's so funny?"

"The Irish gave the bagpipes to the Scots as a joke, but the Scots haven't got the joke yet."

"Better not let the Highlanders hear that. Those big bastards would rip you asunder." Samuel touched Goldie's flanks with his heels. "Make haste. We don't want to miss the battle."

"Don't worry about that. The infantry will fight this one."

The day was deceptively beautiful, with crickets chirping and dragonflies floating over the wildflowers. Birds sang tunefully, so far unperturbed by the blare of the army bands and the thousands of boots pounding through the undergrowth and the harvested fields.

Padraig's words resonated with Samuel. If they were fighting and dying to preserve the wealth of men like Lucan and Cardigan, there was little honor in that. And then there was Lucan's unexplained and continued hostility. What had Samuel done to merit such treatment?

The blast of a bugle yanked him out of his reverie. His Seventeenth Lancers were detaching from the cavalry and heading farther west to guard the left flank. "Let's catch up." He clicked his tongue, and Goldie lunged into a canter. For better or worse, he was a cavalryman, a fighting man. He'd signed up, and now it was time to do his duty. The incompetence of aristocrats like Lucan and Cardigan, and even Raglan, was going to make this a long war with opportunities to win renown, a fame Samuel would use to keep men like Lucan from abusing fellow Irishmen. If he survived.

Samuel intended to survive.

THE END

A WORDS FROM M.J.

Thank you for spending your time reading my first novel! If you enjoyed my book, please consider signing up for my mailing list through the website.

www.mjtwomey.com

HISTORICAL NOTE

In early September 1854, a fleet of over 300 ships transported British and French troops from their disease-ridden camps in Bulgaria to Crimea. On September 14, the troops landed on the beaches of Calamita Bay on the southwest coast of the Crimean Peninsula. The Russians failed to oppose the landing, and within four days all troops, horses, stores, and artillery were onshore. Although there were 8,000 Ottoman troops in the allied army, the French and British considered this principally a French and British war against the Russians.

The allies finally advanced on Sevastopol on the morning of September 19, and despite the long delay, the British troops did not even have time to fill their canteens before marching on a very hot day. The French marched on the right, protected by the guns of the fleet just off the coast. The 8,000 men of the Ottoman army followed them. The British marched inland of the French, exposed on three sides. The Russian commander on the Crimean Peninsula, Prince Alexander Sergeyevich Menshikov, moved his forces west towards the allies, built two embankments, and set up his heavy artillery to repel the British advance.

On the afternoon of September 19, the army reached the

crest of a ridge leading to a gentle valley where the Bulganak River flowed. Raglan sent Lord Cardigan with four squadrons of cavalry to reconnoiter the ground ahead. LordLucan joined them, and they encountered a Russian cavalry force of 2,000. Cardigan calmly ordered his men to form line as the Russians halted. But Raglan found high ground for maximum visibility and saw the of the Russian 17th Division barring the way to the south. Finding Lucan and Cardigan arguing, Quartermaster General Richard Airey ordered the cavalry to retire. That is where I wove in my story that it was Samuel who warned the Light Brigade noy to charge. The action also gained Lucan the ironic but undeserved nickname 'Lord Look-on.'

On September 20, the British-French force reached the Alma River and immediately attacked the Russian positions, but the attacks by British and French were not well-coordinated. The French attacked first and turned the Russian left flank by climbing cliffs that the Russian commander had considered unscalable. Had the British been ready to attack at that point, the Russians might have been routed.

Major-General George Charles Bingham, Third Earl of Lucan, commanded the British Cavalry in Crimea, albeit timidly and poorly. Many Irish hated Lord Lucan and called him "The Exterminator" for his mass evictions in the West of Ireland, where reports say he demolished hundreds of homes and evicted 2,000 people during the Great Famine. Lieutenant-General James Thomas Brudenell, Seventh Earl of Cardigan, commanded the Light Brigade and was Lord Lucan's brothers-in-laws. They despised each other.

The Seventeenth Lancers led the Light Brigade on their fateful charge up the North Valley in the Battle of Balaklava during the Crimean War, but I confess to hijacking their amazing story and imposing my characters among them. Captain William Morris commanded the Seventeenth courageously when they charged, but he was obviously not related to my fictitious

Samuel. The scenes with actual people from these historic events are fiction.

I used the following books for reference:

Palmer, Alan. The Banner of Battle: The Story of the Crimean War (p. 126). Lume Books. Kindle Edition

Sweetman, John. Balaclava 1854 (Campaign). Bloomsbury Publishing. Kindle Edition.

Tarle, Yevgeny. The Crimean War: Volume II. Kindle Edition.

ABOUT THE AUTHOR

M.J. Twomey was born in Ireland and lived in the United States for many years before moving to Central America. He wrote his first fiction when he was 21, before life thrust him onto another path. His adventures as an international yacht racer and professional deep-sea diver provided the hair-rising experiences that allow M.J. to share the raw emotions of fear and conflict with readers. He survived a yacht wreck in the Bay of Biscay and an accident underwater deep below an oil rig in the North Sea. Selling his company several years ago provided M.J. with the time and financial security to write full time.

Printed in Great Britain
by Amazon

56258335R00081